LARS GUSTAFSSON

THE TALE OF A DOG

FROM THE DIARIES AND LETTERS OF
A TEXAN BANKRUPTCY JUDGE

TRANSLATED FROM THE SWEDISH
BY TOM GEDDES

A NEW DIRECTIONS BOOK

Originally published in Swedish as *Historien med hunden* by Natur och Kultur,
Stockholm, 1993. This English translation is published by arrangement with
The Harvill Press, London.

Manufactured in the United States of America
New Directions Books are printed on acid-free paper.
First published as New Directions Paperbook 868 in 1999
Published simultaneously in Canada by Penguin Books Canada Limited

Library of Congress Cataloging-in-Publication Data
Gustafsson, Lars, 1936–
    [Historien med huden. English]
    The tale of a dog: from the diaries of a Texan bankruptcy judge/
Lars Gustafsson: translated from Swedish by Tom Geddes.
        p.   cm.
    ISBN 0-8112-1395-1 (alk. paper)
    I. Geddes, Tom.   II. Title.
PT9876.17.U8H5713   1999
839.73'74—dc21   98–7350
                                                            CIP

New Directions Books are published for James Laughlin
by New Directions Publishing Corporation,
80 Eighth Avenue, New York 10011

"For the creature was made subject to vanity"
Romans 8, 20

"What is man that thou shouldst magnify him?"
Job 7, 17

Contents

Prologue

ON THE MORNING OF Midsummer's Day, which happened to be bakingly hot, I rang my old friend Tony, the District Attorney in Travis County. When I managed to get him on the line, not the easiest thing to do because he is one of the busiest people I know – and with good reason – I admitted that I was personally responsible for a still unsolved and particularly brutal murder that had recently taken place in the area.

Tony listened very attentively and then declared that he had all the suspects he needed in this murder enquiry for the moment. A well-known mass-murderer had just been handed over from up north and was now being questioned about this crime, as well as several unexplained disappearances. He asked me to convey his greetings to my wife, Claire, and assured me that he would of course contact me if it turned out that he required my assistance in the investigation.

For the time being he would prefer to regard my confession as one of the many recent manifestations of my depression that he had heard about. He had been told that I had taken the death of old Professor van de Rouwers surprisingly hard, not least perhaps owing to certain revelations about his activities as a young man in Holland during the War. But I didn't mean, did I, he wondered – with, for the first time during this bizarre telephone conversation, a hint of curiosity in his voice – that I had murdered Professor Jan van de Rouwers too?

"No," I said. "I had nothing to do with his death."

Letters to the Drowning

1. The Film of My Birth

M Y FATHER, A BUILDER in San Saba County, had several hobbies that he pursued with an enthusiasm bordering on fanaticism.

One of them was 16mm cinematography.

I don't know how many cameras and projectors and cutting boards we found after he died. We sold most of them or gave them away. But I still have the films and one of the projectors. The films take up an entire cardboard box right at the back of the capacious wardrobe in the bedroom. There must be at least a hundred, depicting every possible occasion. Myself at seven and my – as far as I can see – happy three-year-old brother at his birthday party. My brother riding on ponies, on round-abouts, myself on the way to my first day at school.

I have to say that quite a few of the films look rather silly. They are dreadfully repetitive, almost as if the filming had been a kind of ritual, an attempt to preserve the memory of a contented family life in all its detail in a rather impersonal fashion. But then there are others that are particularly interesting. In fact I even have access to a film of my own birth. This record of my birth really is especially important to me. I keep it in a separate little container in the big cardboard box. I sometimes project it down in the kitchen when I can't sleep between three and five in the morning. It's much more fun than watching television (the horror films that some channels show at that hour just upset and depress me) or pacing all over the house, looking at a book here and a book there, rubbing at a real or imagined spot on the mahogany table in the living room.

The film of my birth is quite short and has a lot of technical faults. Perhaps the most surprising thing is that a father-to-be was actually allowed to bring photographic floodlights and tripods and the rest of his equipment into a delivery room as early as 1936. Normally fathers were extremely unwelcome in delivery rooms in those days. Most probably my father was a good friend to several of the doctors at the Fredricksburg Centennial Hospital: he used to go fishing with some of them. Fishing was another of his many hobbies.

The pictures of the birth are a very flickering sequence with amateurish lighting, where all the interesting bits are repeatedly hidden by the midwife's back. You can see her white dress, the straps and the belt, everything rather too brightly lit. But then my mother's splayed legs come into view, with my head suddenly starting to push its way out. And the midwife holding me up for my mother to see, still with the umbilical cord attached. And then anonymous hands cutting it.

The whole thing is obscene, frightening and strangely fascinating. I avoid watching it too often, simply because I'm afraid of wearing it out. It's precious to me.

This film is literally the only answer I have to the question: Who am I? Or perhaps I'm mistaken. Perhaps it only tells me where I come from, not who I am. I sometimes ask myself whether it can be about me at all. You never see yourself from the outside to the same extent as when you see your own birth. (I sometimes even ask myself whether my own life is actually about me, and that, as you will realise, is a factor which has left its mark on my story; this tale of a dog, for instance, is not really about me in the slightest. And there is much else too, in the story that follows, that has nothing to do with me whatsoever.)

It would never occur to me to show the film of my birth to anyone else; not to my wife Claire (who doesn't even know it exists), nor to my children (who would be certain to laugh at it: there is no corresponding documentation of their own births). In itself it's absolutely trivial: masses of children are born all the time, every second in fact. But this is very special. It's a statement about myself. That I exist? Maybe.

No. It's also about something else, a mixture of terror and fascination, a terror that is reminiscent of how one felt in boyhood about sex. Something determined that I should exist, something that may have just been chance; something compelled me to be the person I am, to be one specific individual. If my parents hadn't met, that compulsion wouldn't have existed either.

How carefully I try not to fulfil this responsibility that I never sought! And how odd that I identify myself with it! It's not that I would prefer to be dead, I don't mean that. But I would prefer not to have to be a specific individual.

The strange thing is that despite all this the old film of my birth often makes me feel relaxed. I go back up to the main part of the house and on the way to my bed I look into my wifc's bedroom and see her now rather overweight body (which nevertheless belongs to me) as a more solid shadow in the encroaching dawn. Wrapped up again in the warmth of my blankets, I turn on to my side and fall asleep like a child.

2. The Lady in the Bookshop

"THERESA IS HERE NOW," said the surly student. He didn't look very happy about it. I heard the little bell on the door ping. They exchanged a few words. The student was already on his way out, clearly impatient to get to something else, probably a lecture. I hurriedly replaced the book on the shelf (it was about the influence of the planets on our birth) and stepped out from behind the bookshelf that obscured the view to the counter.

I first saw the woman in whose disappearance I was apparently – through no fault of my own – later to play some part, one Thursday in April. It was about two o'clock and I had extended my lunch break from the Court just to be able to talk to her. Absurdly enough about a dog.

She looked exactly as I had imagined: a petite vivacious woman in her upper thirties, wearing a jumper and woollen skirt, much too hot for the time of year I would have thought, with straight dark hair already showing a hint of grey in the front. She had no make-up on and her lips were full but looked as if they lacked passion. Her jumper and skirt covered a slim muscular body. Maybe a jogger or a tennis-player?

Her eyes were a cool blue, perhaps pleased with what they saw. The bookshop is in the rather shabby but agreeable district we call the West Campus, west of the main University area, sandwiched between two of the large, slowly decaying houses still to be seen there. They are always rented out to various groups of students, as is evident from the bicycles chained to the verandah railings. For all I know the bookshop

8

may originally have been a big garage. When I was a student at the University there were far more little bookshops in the city than there are today, new and second-hand. I have no idea why so many should have disappeared.

There were such quantities of books in the shop that it felt as if it would be all too easy to knock over a whole set of shelves, so high and insecure and generally overloaded did they appear. It must have been a bookshop with a very honest clientele, because it didn't seem humanly possible to see what the customers were up to. For a start, I couldn't even find my way to the counter until, turning a corner, I suddenly came upon it.

This was a really enjoyable bookshop. Nearest to the door, presumably as a kind of bait, were the usual old bestseller novels, all of them a few years old and second-hand, of course. Is there anything more dead than a two- or three-year-old bestseller? Then everything changed character completely when you got a bit further in. A very large science-fiction section, bigger than you would normally expect in a campus bookshop. There was even an occasional rarity such as Norman Spinrad's *The Iron Dream* in its original edition, a strange novel about a world in which Hitler as a young man after the fiasco at the Academy of Art in Vienna emigrates to New York, where he becomes a science-fiction author and writes the novel *The Iron Dream*, which is German Nazism in the guise of science fiction. The book never had any great success, since many of the critics misunderstood it as pro-Nazi. This was a copy that had been read until it was almost falling to pieces. Lots of books by somebody I didn't know, Anthony T. Winnicott, but which looked interesting. One of his novels was called *When the Last Human Being Has Died, the Whole Solar System Will Be a Much Safer Hiding Place*. He seemed to have a certain penchant for long titles.

It is said to be a dying art nowadays, I believe, science fiction. I used to enjoy reading it when I was a student. So did my friends. Not because we were particularly interested in technical matters, but because it was a speculative genre of literature in an age that had no time for theology. It kind of fitted in with going to Jan van de Rouwers' lectures. Old Professor Hartshorne's two books on Anselm of Canterbury's Ontological Argument for the existence of God were there too, remarkable works in that they mount a defence of the Argument.

The Old Man – Jan van de Rouwers, whom I'll come back to in due course, but you'll appreciate that I can't possibly write about everything all at the same time – used to examine us on them in his Philosophy course, which was regarded as rather eccentric. Books that dealt with the existence of God were not so popular in the early Sixties. As when? As now? What the devil do I know about how things are now!

A totally disordered collection of theology, Protestant and Catholic all in together, Jewish mystics and the sort of Gnostic gospels that seem to emerge from the sands of the desert nowadays with ever-increasing frequency, jumbled up with peculiar books on healing crystals and the influence of the planets. You could almost imagine that someone had gone out of their way to conceal the interesting books among the uninteresting ones.

And the whole lot had that slight smell of mould that books almost always seem to succumb to in central Texas. Too much humidity. Too much heat. A country that would never be able to keep books for long. That's the dismal truth about Texas. Books don't do well here. They go mouldy.

3. *Whole Foods*

I USED TO DO most of my shopping out where I live, on the other side of the river: in an old shop which is called Tom Thumb at the moment, but which has had many other names. I live in a house right by Town Lake, or Colorado River if you prefer.

I knew just about every assistant there. For a couple of years, until last summer, they had a very pretty student who used to work at the checkout on Sunday evenings, a small dark girl with a somewhat dejected, hunched and deliberate air. Jennifer. I liked her. We often used to have a chat. I always paid at her till. She said she was studying advertising at the University and always helped me out to the car with my bags herself. There was obviously some kind of unexpressed fellow-feeling between us. She disappeared at the end of the spring term. Yes, it must have been last spring. I presume she finished at the University.

All that summer she was my main reason for shopping there on Sunday evenings, a task that otherwise Claire would usually do. Now that the girl's gone I've changed shops. *Mutatio delectat*, as the Romans say. I go shopping in Clarksville instead. It's more or less on my route home in the afternoons or evenings from Court. I always take Seventh Street and Exposition Road anyway as far as the dam that I have to cross, so it's not much of a detour. It gives me an interval of welcome relaxation between work and home. So I've started calling in at Whole Foods some afternoons on the way back from Court.

That's the name of the health-food shop on Lamar Boulevard. It's just below Clarksville, a part of the city up on a hill, where the little white wooden houses were once home to a fine middle-class black population (with washing machines out on the verandah and some still living there; and the *tiny* grocery shop up on the hill still selling paraffin – can there really be houses there without electricity even now?). Clarksville started changing in the early Eighties, in the Seventies in fact. It began when the younger professors at the University noticed that house prices were fairly low there. A few professors appeared among the old black families. Younger ones. Associates.

A little hash, a few co-operatives, piano-teachers and herbalists, lesbian women jogging in pairs in long silk stockings, the characteristic mix of healthy and unhealthy activities of the period. A lawyer, whom I had met occasionally at Court, in my own Court, was found murdered, lying in the boot of his own Jaguar in the garage of one of those elegant condominiums that gradually began to rise up out of the old overgrown gardens like exotic mushrooms. I presume it had something to do with cocaine that hadn't been paid for. But that's just my entirely personal assumption. The cocaine business has no bankruptcy procedures for people who don't want to pay. I sometimes say as a joke that all commercial life would be like the cocaine business if we didn't have regulated arrangements for the suspension of payments and rescheduling of debts.

After the hippies came the yuppies, which was when the expensive condominiums shot up like mushrooms out of the soil. Lawyers, artists and foppish homosexuals of various professions in velvet trousers and cowboy boots. A few young professionals with a bit more money, lawyers and doctors, slipped in at the beginning of the Eighties when some of the builders started erecting the huge smart condominiums up in Clarksville. Spanish palaces and functionalist tower blocks. And Whole Foods, of course, did well out of it all along. I've seen at least three different extensions built. In the Seventies it was a scruffy little co-operative with organic tomatoes and guaranteed toxin-free potatoes on the shelves, and pale red-haired ladies (the kind that always have big dogs waiting in the car), goat's milk and ginseng and very serious young assistants at the checkouts, students and earnest little girls with soft silk ballet shoes in net bags beside their handbags. (I have, I must admit, an interest in supermarket checkout girls that's virtually a hobby, and always have had. Most of them of course are as stupid as cows: spotty, fat and boring lower-class young women. But you constantly come across intriguing exceptions. The very transitoriness of the encounter has a charm in itself. Yes, I keep remembering what Claire often says about my never-fading interest in supermarket cashiers and the women in men's hairdressers, those *gentle priestesses of the fleeting moment*, as I privately call them.)

In recent years Whole Foods has grown in size and become a more cheerful place, as well as noticeably more expensive. But their principles are still intact of course. The pale and, in statistical terms, abnormally thin ladies who stand for ages picking and choosing at the long shelves of vitamins and among the glass bottles of unusual sorts of tea have been joined by the boys in velvet who've been creeping in. But they mostly buy French wines and fuss around the choice grain-fed beef and smoked salmon up at the charcuterie counter – served by the charcuterie assistant's gloved hands, thank goodness – and chat about God knows what in the lengthy queues. Then there are the really delightful young girls in leggings; nowhere else in town can you see so many beautiful figures as in Whole Foods.

What do they do? Modern ballet, perhaps? I've never actually understood what *aerobics* is, though I've always been quite good at Greek. I would guess that the Veuve Cliquot and the well-marbled beef have been biodynamically produced in some mystical way too. Since they're sold here, along with the goat's milk. There was some kind of argument with the authorities about the goat's milk, but I didn't follow it, because I don't drink goat's milk – nor, as far as I'm aware, does anybody else I know.

Over the years the shop has become damnably expensive, but that doesn't seem to have frightened off the health fanatics, and it's probably even been an inducement to the boys in velvet. What is striking is how it has become a meeting place for two different types of people.

The anxious, who worry about vitamins and biodynamic and cholesterol, and the snobs. The anxious, who are easiest to recognise, come because they're afraid that our whole era is poisoning them. They probably also read all the weird magazines, vegetarian and occult, that you see by the checkouts. The snobs, who are a little harder to detect, come because they enjoy food and cooking. And fine wines, of which there are plenty. And to a certain extent they come because the shop has developed into something of a club. They call the cashiers by their first names, and expressions of affection like kisses on the cheek and hugs between customer and cashier are not infrequent. I actually wonder whether the contacts here are more significant than they may appear at first sight. But that's just my own, extremely subjective guess.

Then of course there are ordinary people such as myself. We come because the fruit and vegetables are so good. The tomatoes have a flavour. The apples are wonderful. The wine selection, as I've said, isn't at all bad. Professor Dehlen, my German-born former neighbour who moved to Cherry Lane from the river a couple of years ago because he got rheumatism from living so close to the water, a grand old white-haired university teacher whom I sometimes see there on Fridays, assures me that whoever puts the price labels on the wines makes some rather interesting mistakes from time to time. A *Trockenspätlese* that would cost sixty marks in Berlin will occasionally be going for eight dollars.

So it's quite an entertaining kind of shop. (But it's no

compensation for the relationship I had with that little brunette in my old one.)

What has always fascinated me most is the noticeboard. It's right by the exit and is always filled with slips of paper announcing runaway cats, oriental massage (I wonder a lot about what oriental massage consists of), a lesbian lady seeking a female friend with an interest in canoeing. These little pieces of paper, all in different colours, often provided with tear-off strips with a telephone number that you can take away with you, give a glimpse into other worlds than the one I normally inhabit.

I came across something new the other day, a very tiny note, right at the bottom of the board, fixed with a drawing pin that must have caused its owner's small fingers a lot of problems. It was insecurely pressed in, at an angle:

HAS ANYONE SEEN MY DOG?
The person who took my dog, a wire-haired fox-terrier called Willie, from the street outside Garner & Smiths Bookshop on Guadalupe Street while I was working there last Saturday, is kindly requested to contact me by telephone. The dog needs his medicine, and I really need the dog.

Theresa Biancino. Phone 512–477 68 59
or (work) 512–477 97 25.

On the way out with my two big bags – one of which was pretty awkward, because it really had too many bottles of wine in it – I took a careful look around. Then I tore off one of the strips from the poorly-fastened paper that had Theresa Biancino's phone number on and stuffed it into the breast pocket of my suit. I was in a hurry to get home.

4. Like a Very Watchful Bird

"THERESA IS HERE NOW," said the surly student. I heard the little bell on the door ping. She looked exactly as I'd imagined.

"Yes, I'm Theresa. Is there anything in particular I can help you with?"

She talked fast, her voice betraying a slight unease. It might have been my dark suit that had a rather official look about it. I liked her deep voice. I liked everything about her. Without quite being able to say why.

"I'm the man who rang about the dog that had disappeared."

"Oh, really? Yes, I remember now. It was a couple of weeks ago, of course."

"A wire-haired fox-terrier, called Willie?"

"Yes."

"Who needed his medicine. Theresa, I think I may possibly have some information about a dog."

"You can't possibly have. The dog is dead."

"I know," I said. "Unfortunately I think I killed it. I beat it to death by the side of a dustbin it had pulled over. A fat yellow mongrel."

She looked up with surprise in her eyes. They were very unusual. Greeny-blue, interested and shy. If there was any expression in them, I couldn't detect it. I decided not to go into any further detail.

"Beat it to death?"

"Yes, it was a very unpleasant dog. It dragged out the entire contents of my dustbins, day after day. I couldn't stand it any longer. I have a neighbour who's terribly fussy about his lawn."

"But my dog was a fox-terrier. My dog was run over. The person who ran it over came in a few days later. It was an elderly lady with poor reflexes. She was very upset. I think it would have been worse if it had been a careless student."

"I've never liked telephones," I said. "It's so hard to say anything important to someone you can't see. Otherwise I would have explained myself a bit better on the phone."

"I believe you. You certainly don't look the type who would be capable of beating a poor hungry stray dog to death. But whatever you did to it, it can't have been my dog. My dog was a wire-haired fox-terrier, not a yellow mongrel. And, as I said, it was run over."

She continued gazing at me in the same almost neutral, openly enquiring manner. I came more and more to admire her quick, impatient and at the same time very direct way of interacting with others. There was something proud, almost dismissive about her, like a person who had definitely decided to take care of herself and not ask anyone for help.

I glanced around in search of some way to extend a conversation that logically should already have come to an end.

"Impressive bookshop you have here. I've seldom seen so much good science fiction all under one roof."

"Actually I don't feel entirely at home here. It was my husband who started the shop. And it's his science fiction that I'm trying to sell off. But I can't say it's moving very well just now."

"Is he dead?"

"I don't know, to be honest. I haven't seen him for over three years. I think he's in California. But he's stopped writing letters. He was, what shall I say? – an original."

"Was he very interested in science fiction?"

"You could say that. At least in his own. Which he considered far superior to any other. He wrote science fiction.

Masses of science fiction. But it took him quite a few years before he got much out of it. Sometimes he would do almost a book a month. To pay the rent."

After letting her fine front teeth rest on her lower lip for a moment she added:

"No, he was probably good, but not all that successful."

"What was his name? The same as yours – Biancino?"

"No. He had a completely different name. He wrote under the pseudonym of Anthony Travis Winnicott."

Something told me that it wasn't appropriate to question her much more about this fascinating man. Had he really gone away? Or might he walk in at any moment?

"I don't believe I've read anything of his."

"I was thinking of making some tea now. Would you like a cup?"

"Well, thank you. I've still got a few minutes before I have to get back to the office."

I noticed that she didn't ask where the office was. She wasn't in the least inquisitive – or if she was, it wasn't considered good form in her circles to show it. Her foot, in a very diminutive shoe and a carelessly donned, drooping white sock, was jigging energetically up and down.

"Could you give me a title?"

"Title of what?"

"Of a book by your former husband."

"He's still my husband," she said emphatically. "He's not like the dog. He's not dead."

She was silent for a moment. Her *foot*, on which my attention had focused for some reason, was jigging up and down more and more agitatedly – as if it was trying to prove something.

"Maybe he was a good writer in his way," she said. "Or at least a very stimulating one. But not very easy to have as a husband. Do you know what the book was called that he was writing when he went off?"

"No, I can't guess."

"*Go Quietly! Don't Talk to the Flies!*"

18

"Rather a splendid title, I must say. I've never heard anything like it before."

That too seemed to strike her as a completely new idea. Her face was really quite small, with large, intelligent, but also somehow frightened eyes. At certain instants she reminded me of a very alert, very watchful bird. This watchful, delicate face turned away from me now for a moment (towards the window, towards the damp winter street outside, the light drizzle, the drops of moisture from the Spanish moss on the oak trees bordering her parking space, the occasional passing car); she averted her gaze completely.

And when she turned back to face me it felt almost as if music had begun to play again.

"Yes, indeed. His book titles are often quite funny. One was called *The Return of Anaxagoras*, another *The Clock on the Mountain*. And one about anthropoids, who don't know themselves that they're anthropoids, is called *The Bad Guardians of the Very Secret Conscience*. Yes, there are lots. Did I say that for a while he was writing almost one book a month? It was the only way he could keep himself. Really. How do you keep yourself? Really?"

She smiled her slightly bitter, rather wicked little smile at that "really".

"I'm a bankruptcy judge here in the city."

"That's good. I've been seriously wondering whether the time might be coming to put this shop into liquidation. I'd get sympathetic treatment, I hope?"

"I'm always sympathetic towards everyone who has business in Court," I replied tersely. That was in fact true, it occurred to me as I said it.

"By the way, I knew of course that your dog wasn't the one I killed."

"Do you mean that you really *killed* yours?"

"It wasn't mine. I don't even know whether it belonged to anybody."

"It must have been hungry. Poor dog! Why did you phone, then?"

"Because I was intrigued by your advertisement. I wanted to see what you looked like. I thought you sounded interesting."

"Well – *was* I interesting?"

I gazed long and hard into her eyes, which were now a pale grey-green and very attractive. I was not entirely sure what I could read in them.

5. The Conflagration

THE OLD MAN DIED. Professor Jan van de Rouwers, my former teacher, the great philosopher and semanticist, or, put another way, my neighbour here at the beach, died. At the very beginning of autumn. I think it happened on 15 September.

He probably considered that it was time. That his time had come. The Old Man died and floated down the river. Cruelty, as I've discovered, has great reserves.

Yes. The body, in pyjamas, was found down at the hydro-electricity dam. It had been halted by the grille. Fortunately. They would never have found him if it hadn't been for the fire. He couldn't have known that that very night the entire area down by the Tom Miller Dam would be crawling with fire-boats, men with searchlights, private vessels of all kinds, and the burning, drifting motorboat hulls from Boat Town. It was pure good luck, or bad luck, depending on your point of view.

They would probably never have found him if that criminally neglected and dilapidated collection of boathouses and jetties on the other side hadn't burnt down the same night. It led the rescuers with their boats and searchlights directly to a body that would otherwise have been just an invisible piece of flotsam in the autumn darkness of the river. It would have gone straight through the open storm gates at the next dam.

It's strange when you think about it. What should we have believed? That he had fallen victim to a crime? Or that his own past had perhaps caught up with him? – but wait, I mustn't jump ahead of the story.

Another of my neighbours, young Cliff Jones, who is some kind of computer whizz-kid, which is how he too could afford to buy himself one of these old houses by the beach – even though he got in late – rang me up at ten o'clock in the evening to tell me with great glee that the flames were soaring into the sky and you could hear the powerful costly motorboats exploding one after another as the high-octane fuel in their tanks ignited. He loathed those boats as much as I did. There isn't a single person living here by the beach who doesn't loathe them. The noise creates a disturbance, their wakes are slowly but surely eroding jetties and banks, and they've made it completely impossible to swim over to the wonderful, steep, cedar-clad marble cliffs on the other side, where Claire and I used to swim to when we were happy, young, newly-arrived beach residents.

I went out on to the terrace with my wife, and it really was a magnificent spectacle. You could see flames shooting up at least sixty feet into the night sky, and fire-brigade searchlights shining across the water; the dull explosions from boat after boat were echoing round the hills on our side of the river. According to the *Austin-American Statesman*, which got a short piece into its morning edition the next day, about forty vessels were destroyed. The firemen managed to save some that were moored on the outside by towing them into deep water. They had also towed out some of the burning boats. The chief fire officer didn't think the sunken wrecks would cause any damage to the ecology of the lake. Arson was not suspected – it had all begun on a slipway where the recently-repaired boats were left.

For anyone familiar with the site it would come as no surprise. There wasn't a marina in the city that was so criminally neglected. Old boxes of empty bottles, oil-soaked rags, discarded mooring ropes on the narrow jetties between the boats. And the owner himself, that perpetually grinning man with his icy blonde woman as office assistant – the place had been heading for disaster. I took my old cabin cruiser there as recently as the early Eighties, so I know what I'm talking about.

It's not easy to guess what could have caused the fire. A tramp tossing a cigarette-end carelessly into a barrel of dirty rags, maybe. Or someone who didn't approve of motor boats. There are many who don't. Here on this side it was certainly not just Cliff who was overjoyed. Our little jetties and old-fashioned boathouses don't have an easy time in summer when the water-skiers zoom past, in relentless succession, at about thirty or forty knots. The piles lose their footings because the lake-bed around them is churned up and disturbed by their wake, boats are damaged, and you can hardly even sit down on the jetty (which has always been my Sunday relaxation) with *The New York Times* and a cup of tea.

So you can say that the conflagration was also a good thing. You could in fact say what the prophet Isaiah said about God, that He created both good and evil.

One advantage is that there'll be forty motorboats fewer next summer, if they don't get themselves replacements by then, of course. It'll be possible to enjoy a morning coffee on the jetty again, in the shade of the big willow trees. The black herons, the ducks and the pelicans will have a more peaceful breeding season perhaps, and the jetties will last longer. And another thing is that they found Jan van de Rouwers' body before it slipped into the power-station turbines. It was obviously the light of the burning wrecks that helped them find him. (*A mini Pearl Harbor*, Cliff said on the telephone; there's really no limit to how cynical young people can sound.)

Dr Jan van de Rouwers' disappearance had nothing to do with the conflagration. Not with the conflagration as such. Not with fire as such. His final element was water. Perhaps water was always his element. He must have dived in from his jetty a night or two earlier and floated downstream. It's not the first time something like that has happened. The river, the Texas

Colorado River – which is not to be confused with the other one which is even bigger – the river is big enough as it is, and has seen it all before. Not just once, but many times. It used to be smaller. Before the extensive dam projects came with President Roosevelt's Federal unemployment programme in the Thirties. That was when the Mansfield Dam was built. We live on the stretch of the river between Mansfield Dam to the north and Tom Miller to the south. In Lake View Café, in the bar, over there on the other side, there are some old framed photographs showing how it used to look before the Mansfield Dam was constructed. Phenomenal spring floods with wooden houses and uprooted trees and boats all floating around one another in a single huge swirling mass.

Sometimes when I drive over the dam, on the narrow ledge soaring about two hundred and fifty feet above the lower lake, I wonder what would happen if the dam *burst*. An ideal target for a bomb, as the owner of the Shell petrol station on the other side frequently says. He was a bomber pilot in the Second World War and has an eye for that sort of thing.

Well, we don't have to be afraid of the Russians now. But there are still terrorists, of course. If the dam were blown up, the water escaping from Lake Travis, which is nothing but a great reservoir, would take us all with it. We wouldn't have time to get out of our houses. The headlights of the fleeing cars would disappear beneath the surface and the beams would turn a deeper and deeper green until they were extinguished beneath the enormous volume of water.

That's what Steve says, the man who runs the Shell station on the other side of the dam. He's seen things like that, he says, when he bombed dams in Germany in 1944. I'm not altogether sure that I believe him. I mean, I believe him, but I don't believe he's seen it himself. He's too young. His story is too much like a scene from television.

It often strikes me nowadays, when I'm sitting with men a bit older than myself, in my club, The Town and Gown, for instance, and they start reminiscing about their experiences in the Second World War, that it's really the old black-and-white documentary films from cable television's Educational Channel 9 that they're recounting. They think they've experienced it themselves.

In fact people in general today seem to find it hard to distinguish between what they've experienced themselves and what they've just dreamt or seen on television.

6. *Vegetarian Journey*

D O WE REALLY HAVE any friends, Claire and I? That's actually not a very easy question to answer. Sometimes it seems as if we have, dozens of them. They come a couple of times a year and fill the entire terrace. We're hunting for plastic cocktail glasses in the bushes for weeks afterwards. I don't understand why they can't keep a check on them, or is it the wind that blows them away? The guests arrive with presents in neat little packages. For the children's birthdays, occasionally for our wedding anniversaries. There's a general hubbub and lots of conversation, the ladies show off their new cocktail dresses and chat about who's expecting babies, the men discuss lawns and bank business and a new country club in North West Hills with much better tennis courts. It all looks tremendously lively and sociable, and the whole street is full of parked cars.

But if you think about it you have to ask yourself whether they're real friends at all. Most of them are from banks that have dealings with the Court, and some are members of the old, commercially orientated law firms. There are names that I've known for three generations, and, counting back in time, have even caught a glimpse of the fourth before it disappeared. And a few friends of Claire that she's kept up with since her schooldays. They're the quietest of all. Have I really no friends? That's nonsense. George and I went through practically all the schools here in the city together, from Anderson High School to the University of Texas School of Law. Admittedly he was at Cambridge, in England, for a couple of years as a Marshall Scholar reading Philosophy, while I started on a doctorate here, that I subsequently gave up, in the Philosophy of Religion. Otherwise we've kept up with one another quite well. Funnily enough it was he, out of the two of us, who became a patents lawyer, yet I was the one who was always interested in trademarks and patents when we began our legal studies. We thought it was slightly artistic. At Greasy Tile – as we called the place where we started out, a dreary little firm that had achieved the amazing feat of creating chambers in which none of the rooms had windows – a little artistry was indeed required, as one can imagine. He has his own firm now but I don't know how well it's doing. He travels a lot anyway. All over the world. Trademarks have to be separately registered in every country.

I don't know how he manages it.

Somewhere along the way he has become a vegetarian. A totally committed vegetarian. Of course the papers nowadays are full of cholesterol warnings: you can't go into a grocery shop without finding a woman in a corner wearing a white coat and taking it upon herself to test your cholesterol level. You hear of families where little children have stopped growing because they're not getting enough cholesterol. Do they think that three-year-olds are at risk of heart attacks? My old physician Dr Cohen says it's all a load of nonsense. It's not cholesterol but oestrogen, it's the sex hormones that play the decisive role in whether or not you have a heart attack one day. Statistics prove it, he says. The age of heart attacks in women begins ten years later than in men, and that's because they retain their oestrogen for ten more years. If you want to avoid heart attacks you should keep up your sex life. That's not what Dr Cohen says, but that's the conclusion I've drawn myself. (I keep my own going very successfully with the aid of these delightful young supermarket cashiers and hairdressers who seem to be placed in my path almost exclusively for that purpose.) So actually it depends on just one factor, either cholesterol or oestrogen. The stupidity of it is that these people think they've found the answer to death. It's a complete riddle to me why they should want to live for ever; their lives seem so utterly boring and devoid of meaning. The more meaning-less the life, the more people seem to want to hold on to it. It's young, beautiful, fit people who do dangerous things, weaving their motorcycles in and out of traffic lanes or mountaineer-ing. It's unappetising blue-rinsed old ladies who carry on about cholesterol and all that stuff.

George is a big, heavily-built, blond man, who works all the time and never gets home before eight in the evening. I pre-sume he's exactly the kind of person who could easily have a heart attack. But his vegetarianism has nothing to do with that. He's a vegetarian on moral grounds; he abhors the idea that we persist in killing and cutting up masses of innocent animals to keep ourselves alive. He detests the smell of meat and says he sometime feels quite nauseous when fifty aircraft passengers simultaneously open their containers of liver pâté. His wife is the same. He has convinced her. They have no children. If they had, I would have wondered a great deal about what would happen when the children grew up to be strong hefty baseball-playing teenagers, sneaking off at dusk to school-friends' homes begging to be allowed to join in their barbecues and sink their teeth into the leftovers of their friends' steaks. (Football is no longer played among the better classes.) Would they be punished? Or be sent to the school psychiatrist? Thank goodness for their sakes that these children don't exist. (Yet another reason to infer that that damned Anselm of Canterbury was mistaken in his very first premise. *Of course*: it's *so* much more dignified not to exist than to exist.)

The worst thing about it, admittedly, is that you can understand his point of view. You only have to shift your perspective for a moment, so to speak, and you can sympathise with it. But we never say that to George. I ask provocative questions instead. What would we do with all the dead animals if no one would eat them? Can you imagine a cemetery for cows and bulls, mass graves for pigs? But, he says, if nobody ate meat, there wouldn't be any need for the enormous stock of animals we have in Texas. So you mean it's better for the animals never to have been born than to be born to be hygienically slaughtered in an abattoir, say I. What do you mean by *hygienically*, he asks, looking at me with his big blue eyes. This of course is just circling round the real question.

I notice that I'm finding it hard to come to the point. I don't know why, but since the Old Man died, I've been a little absent-minded.

Anyway, we had farmed out our children one summer weekend in the early Seventies to some other friends so that we could drive to Port Aransas on Padre Island with George and his wife Annette. In order, we said, to have a good rest. People say that Port Aransas is not the same as it used to be. Hotels have spread out further across Padre Island. The chemical industries along the coast, which weren't there at the beginning of the Sixties when I was a hippie and used to smoke marijuana on the warm night sand with fellow-students and girlfriends, can no longer be trusted. Piles of brown seaweed blow up on to the beaches, more than can be cleared away. It's said to be something to do with the earth's atmosphere getting warmer. "Greenhouse effect" is the expression. Next to cholesterol, the greenhouse effect is what the newspapers are mostly writing about in 1990. The greenhouse effect is another name they think they've found for death.

We set off, as far as I remember, one Friday morning, very early. It must have been about five o'clock when George swept into our drive in his jeep. He had one of those new jeeps with four-wheel-drive that look a bit too comfortable inside. You can live in them. But we had booked two adjacent condominiums in Port Aransas, right by the beach. When we were students we used to sleep on the sand out there, with our girlfriends. I think it must have been for old times' sake, to relive those memories, that we had decided to go there.

There isn't much of me that's awake at five o'clock in the

morning – I'm pleased at that hour of the day if I know what I'm called and where I live, but George and his wife looked as fresh as daisies. "Hello," they said, "have you had breakfast?" The idea that you could eat breakfast at five o'clock in the morning is of course completely foreign to me: two headache tablets and a cup of strong coffee is about all I can think of at that time of day. I've forgotten to say that I've always had a high regard for George's wife. She's a petite little ginger-haired girl; no, she isn't any more. She's grey now and rather plump, but in the Sixties she was small, dainty and ginger-haired.

Her name is Annette and she was my girlfriend before George took her over. Full breasts, a lot of enthusiasm, very nice. She's a naturally emotional type, but used to keep it under control in the Sixties by getting involved in various *movements*. What she does with her emotions nowadays, I have no idea. I sometimes feel I would like to sleep with her again, just once maybe. To remind myself of something. But there probably won't be much chance of that.

Anyway, we started out for Port Aransas, that morning in the Seventies. We threw in our suitcases and kissed one another on the cheek, put on the radio and drove east out of Texas Hill Country and on to the great plain that becomes flatter and flatter the nearer you get to the sea. It's an extremely long drive; it takes a whole day.

Needless to say, by about eleven o'clock even I was beginning to feel hungry. "Shall we have a little lunch now?" I suggested. "Where?" said George. "There'll no doubt be a McDonalds in the next place we come to," I said. "Hamburgers?" said George, almost as if I'd made him some kind of shameful proposition. "Sure," I replied. A strained silence fell. It took me a moment to realise why. Vegetarianism had struck again.

"So, what do you suggest?" I asked. "We can wait," he said. "You can have hamburgers. We'll sit in the car and listen to the radio while you go." Strange idea of fun. Ah well. So there we sat twenty minutes later in a McDonalds. Claire and myself, eating hamburgers. George and Annette sitting in the car drinking chlorinated water out of paper cups, we assumed. You only have as much fun as you make.

And as they sat there drinking their highly-chlorinated and extremely unhealthy McDonalds' water out of paper cups, they were gazing out on the world with their big blue ingenuous eyes. (One could imagine.) While we sat inside in order not to upset them with our bestial McDonalds' odours. And their big blue ingenuous eyes were striving to express neither reproach nor approval. Just an unspoken indication that we and they didn't really quite belong to the same world, but could be friends anyway. Or perhaps we couldn't?

Well, eventually Claire and I came back to the car, hoping we didn't smell too much of large dead animals. Of course we did all we could to avoid showing that we felt slightly harassed, or even on trial. That *neutral* look from people I know are actually critical always disturbs me more that I can say. I see it in Court occasionally, and there you simply have to put up with it.

But from friends? Perhaps it has something to do with my parents? Did my father use to look at me like that? I don't know. I don't remember at all, quite honestly, how he used to look. Did he ever look at me?

Anyhow, we arrived in Port Aransas at nightfall and found the hotel without too much trouble. It was the modern type of beach hotel where the guests stay in bungalows which even have kitchens and kitchen utensils, but it was much too late of course to start preparing a meal. On both sides of the narrow promontory the waves were breaking soothingly on sandy beaches that had been partially cleared of seaweed brought up by the last storm. We went into the dining room, a quite ordinary hotel dining room, it has to be said, with a long and surprisingly expensive menu. With lots of Mexican food. I hate Mexican food because it always seems to consist of mushy beans and makes me feel so dreadfully heavy and glutinous that I can hardly move after eating it.

OK, vegetarian, why not! I thought. Anything's better than Mexican beans mashed into a sort of brown gruel and wrapped in thick doughy discs of wheat that burn your throat. "Let's be vegetarians just for one evening at least, Claire," I said.

So there we were – the whole little gang – sitting down with a colourful plate of salad and a small glass of wine each.

Salads take ages to eat. I presume that's why cows don't have much time for anything except eating. We had a gentle, leisurely conversation about various things. About law firms and their idiosyncrasies. About the fast-growing real-estate market in Texas at that period, wondering whether we should have become real-estate agents instead. Lord, they were hopeful times. That was when the beaches on the other side of the lake started to become infested with new palatial villas, and when everybody wanted to join a country club. Wine merchants and country clubs flourished. It was kind of fashionable to be refined for a while. I met George in the street the other day and congratulated him on our not having gone into the real-estate business then after all. (Whether he is still a vegetarian is something I don't know, but it's pretty safe to assume he is.)

George has a client who until recently had an office of forty people and capital of over three hundred million dollars. Right now this client can't afford to pay his lawyer's fees. George often mentions him. The man has obvious difficulties in understanding his situation, in grasping that there literally isn't anything left. Exactly like some patients who have been paralysed in traffic accidents and simply cannot comprehend that they will be confined to a wheelchair for the rest of their lives. They believe that everything will suddenly change for the better. George's client believes in precisely the same way that he will soon have his three hundred million back. As soon as his bankruptcy is over he'll start up in business again, find new benevolent bank managers and interesting new tracts of land that can be exploited as real estate. He can't see that the banks that were recently so benevolent to him now have new owners and new boards, and that his visiting card is one they immediately cast into the wastepaper basket even if he has it sent in on a gold tray. George says his client just doesn't want to hear any such arguments. He still goes on refusing to get himself an ordinary honest job, and spends days in the rather seedy little rented room in the southern suburbs where he's living at the moment, trying to devise fantastic new business schemes. From what George has heard, he's also smoking a lot of marijuana, but the question of course is where he's getting the money from. From hidden reserves, perhaps. It's well known that hidden reserves are hardly uncommon in Texan bankruptcies. What I'm talking about is that inability to perceive when you're really skating on thin ice: we don't need to be real-estate speculators to be afflicted by it. *I too have been skating, or standing (like a funny comic-strip character), on thin ice for some time.* Where are my hidden reserves?

Anyway, in those days we were still fairly young and we sat there over our salads trying to be broad-minded and tolerant (now we would say "politically correct"), which we interpreted as meaning that everybody should probably be vegetarian.

We were altogether too weary after the long drive to tuck into our salads with any real zest. We went off to our respective rooms. And of course we woke up at two o'clock in the night ravenously hungry. Since there was nothing but ice cubes, Claire and I had to allay our hunger by drinking almost half each of the bottle of bourbon I'd brought for the whole holiday, and on that diet we both soon managed to get a thumping headache.

If we had been in the city we would probably have jumped into the car and driven to an all-night store, but that's not very easy to do out there among the sand-dunes. And naturally the last ferry to the mainland had gone. But we lay there,

Claire and I, in each other's arms, almost on the verge of tears, talking about how bad the world can be. There are no sexual pleasures for those who are very hungry and also have a headache from too much whisky.

I still find it incredibly hard to understand how vegetarians survive. There's no food in their food. But I can't really see why we got so terribly angry that night. After all, it was our own fault. Before the sun rose we had made our plans for exactly how we would pack and get away from there to another hotel somewhere else, just to escape the horrific vegetarian pressure. Things didn't work out quite like that, needless to say. In the morning we made our excuses a little distractedly and rushed off to a grocer's, where we laid in a substantial stock of our usual old food. After all, we had a kitchen. We enjoyed a proper breakfast of bacon and eggs. (In my parents' house we were so Jewish that we avoided pork; typically for the majority of modern American Jews we no longer bother about such things. What Hitler didn't achieve, modern American food conformity will bring about: the final demise of Jewishness, in completely undramatic and unbloody ways, through mixed marriages and bacon for breakfast.)

We didn't see much of George and his wife for the rest of that weekend. There was a kind of unspoken agreement between us not to meet at mealtimes, but since we went off in different directions, we didn't see much of one another the rest of the time either. If they were down at the sea, we were in the swimming pool, and vice versa. By Sunday afternoon we had already started avoiding each other to some extent. We remained friends. As I've said, I still enjoy chatting with him in the street when we meet, and I've always liked his wife. But I have a strong feeling that on that occasion we lost meaningful contact with those particular friends once and for all. As if by tacit agreement we stopped getting together in the same spontaneous way as before. Stopped playing tennis, stopped phoning on Fridays to ask whether we should go to the theatre or cinema together. Which we used to do.

No, we haven't got any real friends, Claire and I. That's always been the case, and I often wonder why. I have something else instead, that I like to call my *shadows*. Windy is a typical shadow of mine. The girl in the supermarket was a shadow, elusive yet friendly. Theresa, my strange little bookseller over on West Campus, is another.

7. Windy's Story

SHALL I TELL YOU a story? An even nastier story? Oh, I'll tell you as many as you like. What could be easier than telling nasty stories?

Windy is the name of the girl who cuts my hair. (A bankruptcy judge can't have long hair – unless he's a woman, of course.) She's a tall, fat, bulky red-head, and so short-sighted that she has to lean very close over me to compare both temples and see whether she's trimmed them equally short on both sides. Her sad, blue, myopic eyes look into mine with constant and unwavering desire; I can sense the heavy breathing beneath her soft breasts. And all the time she's cutting my hair she tells me the most extraordinary stories.

I don't need to say much to keep her conversation going. I imagine it's pure nervousness that makes her talk. If she couldn't do that, she'd . . . do what? Anyway, the stories are quite remarkable. I suspect that she gets them from those incredible magazines of sensational exaggeration and lies that you see at the checkouts in supermarkets just as you're on your way out. *The National Enquirer* and that sort of thing. I've never dared buy any of them, since I always buy my groceries in a Tom Thumb in the district where I live (except when I go to Whole Foods, but they're so healthy of course that they don't stock them; they have magazines on organic lifestyles instead). But the headlines usually rivet my attention so completely that in the end the cashier has to prompt me to step forward with my purchases.

JACKIE KENNEDY
EXPECTING CHILD BY ALIEN
FROM OUTER SPACE

SEVEN-YEAR-OLD REGULARLY
ATE COCKROACHES
MOTHER IN DESPAIR

SLEEPING MONSTER
WEARING ROLLER SKATES
FOUND IN CAVE

FULLY PRESERVED FEMALE BODY
OBSERVED BY ASTRONAUTS
ON MOON

I wonder what sort of people write those articles. Do they enjoy it? Or do they feel resentful that they haven't got jobs on better-class newspapers where they could be "seeking out the truth" instead? I increasingly feel that I know very little about other people. How can Windy, for instance, be so interested in these stories? Are there thousands of people reading these strange fabrications? We don't have just one, but many different cultures, and they seem to have so little to do with one another. There must be other whole types of literature around the corner that I have no concept of. Or am I mistaken? Does she invent her stories herself?

She rubs the shampoo into the roots of my hair with her strong vigorous little fingertips, trying to elicit from the hairdressing procedure all the modest erotic and sensual qualities it has to offer. For some reason she often says she *has been thinking about me* when I turn up in the salon. I sometimes wonder what she means by *thinking about me*.

She reads the daily newspapers, anyway. Windy has two children and is divorced for the second time. She always describes marriage as a dreadful institution. She talks about the children a lot. She's bought a second-hand computer for the older one and she's thinking of sending the younger to a summer camp in August. It's expensive and she doesn't know where she'll get the money from. Her second husband, who is apparently some sort of travelling salesman for a tool firm, bought a house way out in the country, somewhere in the direction of Wimberley. He seems to have more or less *parked* her there. His visits became less and less frequent. The house, she says, was in a fairly isolated spot. The worst time was when she was expecting the second baby and had to keep an eye on the four-year-old on a piece of land full of bottomless old wells with rotting wooden covers, fire ants and the occasional quietly rustling but deadly rattlesnake in the tall dry winter grass, where a child would never have a chance to see it before it was too late.

"Not that anything ever actually *happened* there," she went on. "It was the fact that nothing happened that made me so uneasy. It was like a horror film on TV just before the horrors begin. But that's how it was *the whole time*. I didn't even have a car that would start every day. The battery would run down, so I had to phone my nearest neighbour to get it going. It was a miserable old man I used to ring, who lived on the next hill straight across the valley. He became a bit more unwilling on each occasion. Whichever way I looked there were just cedar-clad hills and a dust-cloud or two rising from a track. I could see a car coming up the track half an hour before it arrived. But I never knew whether it was Dan or somebody else.

"When the water pump stopped or one of the children got measles, it felt as if my heart almost stopped too. When I got help it was sometimes very strange help. People often turn strange when they realise you're a woman on your own a long way from anywhere in a dilapidated house on a hill. It was an electrician who almost raped me.

"But what do you do when you've got small children to look after? Having that responsibility is not as easy as you'd think," she continued, at the same breathless, almost breakneck, speed.

"Did you see that frightening story on *Sixty Minutes* the other day? The one about children in Alaska?"

"No. I have too much to read to find time to watch TV. I let my wife take care of that. She tells me about it sometimes, if there's anything important. What children in Alaska?"

"Shall I trim the hair inside your ears, too? It's funny: all men over forty get a lot of stiff little hairs in their ears. Most of my customers want me to snip them off."

"Yes, for God's sake, cut them off. Don't you remember, we cut them last time? But what about the children in Alaska?"

"It was in all the newspapers! It was definitely not just in *Sixty Minutes*. Some time in the spring. When it happened. Well, I'll tell you," says Windy, pushing back a lock of red hair from her forehead so that I can see into her big blue unwavering eyes again. "I'll tell you: 1982, or thereabouts, or maybe a bit earlier, when the great boom hit Alaska, masses of people went up there, building workers etcetera, from other States. Yes, even from Texas. They were the ones who built the big oil pipelines, the sort of people who live in caravans and portable cabins. And they settled at various building sites and were doing all right until the boom suddenly came to an end in the mid-Eighties. Then they took their things with them and disappeared south again. Nothing special about all that. *Except that some of them couldn't be bothered to take their children with them when they left.* Can you imagine it? Moving on and just leaving your children behind you, teenagers and little ones alike?"

"Unbelievable!"

"Yes, isn't it? Shall I take a fraction more off here? At your temples? I think straight white sideburns like this look nice and dignified."

"Yes, they do."

"How very convenient for them! Just dump them. But then gradually it was discovered, in the schools first of all, that the children had simply been left behind. They didn't give a damn about them. Loads of adolescents and younger children who suddenly one day had nowhere to go after school. In an icy cold, snowy climate, where snowploughs thunder along the roads from early morning on, and the smoke rises absolutely straight and blue as dusk falls at about one o'clock in the afternoon."

"You talk about it so graphically, Windy. I mean so that it's really easy to imagine it. I could almost believe you'd been there."

"Yes, I've lived there too. For a while. When I was married to my first husband, the plumber. Yes, that must have been at the beginning of the Eighties too. Well, it was only for a short period. But just think, Judge Caldwell, just imagine a child like that, a thirteen-year-old, maybe somewhat scruffy, not particularly well looked after by the parents, with a runny nose and wet gloves and a quilted jacket that's far too thin, getting off the school bus in the evening, with a few dog-eared comics and the remains of a sandwich in his bag. Is that OK now? Perhaps a bit shorter in the front? He gets off the school bus and goes into the campsite, under the sodium lamps, the usual path between those portable homes. Made so that they only take an hour or two to hoist them up on a trailer and drive away with them. So the boy goes along under the sodium lamps, the snow is falling, he's hungry and glad to be home. But where his parents' portable cabin should be there's now only a big black rectangle in the snow, the place where the house used to stand, a little darker because there hasn't been time for it to snow so much there as round about. And that's all. His parents have simply deserted him. He stands there, with a school bag full of comics that he's just swapped on the bus, and that's all he owns now, a dishevelled, perhaps slightly frightened, but nevertheless quite happy little boy coming home from school to discover that his parents and even the house itself, the only home he's ever had or known, have gone. There's absolutely *nothing there*! What should he do? What, in all his desolation, can he do? Is there anything to reassure him of his very existence? Everything that until then had substantiated it is gone!"

(I am often surprised by Windy's enormous eloquence, when she *gets going*, as it were, gets into her stride, is absorbed and carried along by the story she's telling. I've never heard such eloquence in my own Court.)

"He starts searching?"

"Yes indeed. He starts searching, the poor boy. Shall I take a bit more off in the front? It's very nice thick hair you have, Judge Caldwell. Thick for your age. Well, what I mean . . ."

"Yes, that's fine, Windy, but please go on with the story."

"OK, Judge Caldwell. We'll carry on then, though it's horrible. The boy searches wildly hither and thither. Since all the portable cabins are so damned alike, there's always the hope – at least for the first hour – that he's somehow gone astray. Maybe the school bus dropped him off too soon? He looks to the north and he looks to the south. But that makes it all the more obvious to him that everything is the same as usual. The trees are the same. The neighbouring cabins are the same. The neighbours themselves are the same. The only thing that's different is the snow-free rectangle where his parents' house used to stand, supported on twelve-inch posts that are still lying around here and there in the rectangular patch. He picks one up and weighs it in his hand as if it were secreting the answer.

"But it isn't. He throws it out into the snow, where it sinks and disappears from view. The neighbours are rather embarrassed. They don't really know anything. They weren't at home when it happened. Would he like a glass of water, perhaps? A Coca-Cola? They offer him dinner. Yes, of course they do. They offer him dinner. But rather uneasily. They give one another sidelong glances. What next? Will this child have to stay with them? But that wasn't really what they wanted when they asked little Jeff to come in and warm his hands. Should they phone the Sheriff? But the boy hasn't done anything wrong. It's never a good idea to call in the Sheriff for matters such as this. They might even be suspected of having something to with it.

"'He's welcome to come and eat here for a few days, but then we'll have to make it clear to him that he must take care of himself after that.'

"The boy thanks them for the meal. He goes out. It's a cloudless night. The stars are large and bright, the air is cold and his breath steams. He goes out beneath the stars and doesn't know where he's going to sleep; he has his entire life before him and he really doesn't know anything, least of all what he's going to do next."

Yes, that's how she goes on, does Windy. As I emerge on to the street my mind is still reeling somewhat from her stories. But also from the sensation of her soft, sensitive, nervous fingertips that always finish off by massaging the nape of my neck. (I'm never terribly good at remembering where I left the car.)

I walk very slowly down through the whole area and right through the whole of the Faculty Club car park (the traffic wardens don't often bother me: I have *Federal Judge* on my number plate) pensively hunting for my car, not knowing what to make of the boy in Alaska. Later, in the lift, I see familiar and unfamiliar faces, judges and secretaries and lawyers all intermingled, talking of matters both trivial and weighty, about nail varnish and bankruptcy cases, while I myself am just worrying about what to make of the boy in Alaska. Only when I'm back in my own study, as I cross the worn "oriental" carpet and head for the waiting piles of papers on the large cheap brown desk, do I realise that the boy in Alaska must be seventeen years old by now. What can he have been doing all these years?

8. Conscience Has Many Grey Days

THE OLD MAN DIED.
I've already said that.
And then that business about the dog.

Seeing how helpless, ugly and completely insignificant that dog was when dead, I started to wonder. How could I have been angered by it to that degree? Such suppressed feelings, of irritation, of rage, and if only I knew at what.

The great fat, disgusting yellow body of the dog, limp and lifeless in the black plastic bag. That's how we'll all look one day. But I hope not like this dog, with its skull crushed and one eye hanging out of its socket, and bright red foam in the corners of its mouth. I must have smashed and beaten really violently with the edge-trimmers that happened to be at hand. It was lucky that both those things were to hand that day: the edge-trimmers and the big black plastic bag for garden rubbish. It was rubbish he was after, wasn't it?

And the summer was gradually coming to an end, too. The Old Man died, you could say, at the right time of year.

In October the river swells and turns brown and fast-flowing. The power station above lets through more water, ice-cold deep water from the bottom of Lake Travis that becomes surface water here. No more bathers. Nowhere near so many water-skiers, even in the years when their boats have not been burnt. Algae don't do very well in the colder water from the depths, so they die off too.

The herons sit in large groups in the trees, undisturbed, as serious as Odin's ravens.

I came to this side of the lake eighteen years ago. It was Claire who wanted to live by the water; she wanted to live where she wasn't surrounded by other houses. In Tarrytown, among all the grand houses beneath the oaks, she felt a bit hemmed-in sometimes, she says. With all those women in tennis dresses that they never wore for playing tennis but only to show off to one another when they drove their children to nursery school, strange women who looked somehow desiccated even when young, women with hard lines round their mouths that gave such clear evidence of their husbands' sexual incompetence – or perhaps lack of interest. Jeeps and joggers and dogs and cyclists and the little dark-skinned men who were constantly ringing at the door and wanting to weed the garden or mend the roof and whom you couldn't really be sure of. (Were they looking for a little gardening job or just reconnoitring for a burglary?)

Claire has always felt a bit claustrophobic, I think, when she's crowded together with others and has to greet her neighbours every morning. I know few people who have such little need of others as she does. The question is whether she needs me either, now that the children are grown up and married and gone.

The Old Man, Jan van de Rouwers, came here much earlier. He came from Harvard at the end of the Fifties. He had arrived at Harvard from Hamilton College in New York Upstate via New York, as a refugee from Europe. Apparently an extremely brilliant young academic and refugee. Our Dean, who must have been the illustrious Silver who subsequently went to Boston University, probably relied greatly on our lake to tempt various people here that he wanted to add to the Faculty. The then-crystal-clear spring water at Barton Springs and Texas' friendly little Colorado River with all its dammed-up lakes: Lake Buchanan, immense and mysterious, for eagles; Lake Travis for sailors; Lake Austin for motorboats and wonderful beach villas with boathouses and jetties; and furthest south City Lake, where you can only paddle canoes. And in the spring all those hundreds of thousands of fireflies in the dense foliage of the shore-line cliffs. Showers of green sparks to fire the imagination. It sometimes looks as if it were some kind of electrical disturbance in the film of reality.

This Dutchman, whom I've already gone on about so much, arrived here straight after the War. He was not as renowned then as he was later to become.

The house where he was still living just a couple of weeks ago, alone for the last few decades as far as I understand, with the exception of the odd PhD student or young female professor who would move in for a while, only to move out equally abruptly and leave no trace, was quite spectacular. In its way. The whole thing was made of wood, built on several levels, airy, almost as if suspended. Parts of it in fact projected over one of those little channels that run from the river. Certainly costly: experimental and spacious. Very much a house of the Fifties, from the late, slightly precious Fifties.

Probably rather tiring for an old man. It had, as I recall, an inordinate number of staircases everywhere. His library, which was extensive, was in the part that hung over the water. He must have sat there writing with the weird feeling that time was running away beneath him. Easy to reach from the shore of the lake; it takes just ten minutes by fairly speedy motorboat to get into town. I don't know whether Van de Rouwers ever made use of that possibility. I often did so in the days when boat fuel was reasonably cheap. Had an old car parked by one of the moorings on the other side. It's lovely to travel by water, especially after work. It clarifies the thought processes. In my curious profession you need to clean out your thoughts occasionally.

It's good simply to get out of the Court and its stuffy air (though I often recommend ventilating the room)! On the days when the proceedings are on a Clause 13 rescheduling, the room has an atmosphere of poverty, bitterness, and not infrequently a fear so strong that it literally steams up the windowpanes. Lawyers from the large firms in smart suits, clients with vulgar gold watches on their wrists, wrinkled old farmers with callused hands who don't really comprehend the whole procedure, nervous young couples (almost always white; they are the only ones with loan debts because they are the only ones to get loans from the banks) who have brought along one, two, sometimes up to three, fidgety children that they try to keep quiet as best they can – all of them sooner or later have to engage my attention.

Yes, I'm a bankruptcy judge, and thus a Federal judge. It's probably fair to say I have an adequate amount of what's called "qualifying experience". I know my job. I was a bankruptcy lawyer in a big firm here in town for sixteen years before I became a judge.

I remember the Old Man being very interested. He wondered how I could carry on for so long with something like that. He probably meant: without getting bored by it. He wondered what I was doing there at all.

I explained to him that in the real world someone has to take decisions.

He couldn't accept that.

So I used to tell him that bankruptcy law generates enormous numbers of intellectual problems. Clause 11, I said, is in principle as good at teasing out subtle distinctions as Anselm's Ontological Argument for the existence of God.

He laughed at that. He had a long-standing peculiar weakness for Anselm of Canterbury's Ontological Argument for the existence of God. Always liked to include it in his courses on the History of Philosophy, would refer to it even in his normal everyday conversation. Which may be justified by the tremendous influence it had on the history of ideas and ontological problems, but which nevertheless might seem a trifle quaint as a hobby. You felt there was something obsessive in his relationship to Anselm's Argument and all its variants, that he must be going around thinking about it *the whole time*.

I actually took one of his famous Introduction to

Philosophy courses in the last year before I went over to Yale and Law. He lived up to his reputation. He was indeed a magnificent teacher. But he was no longer playing his most provocative tricks then, because he was a bit older. Only half-a-dozen years before, he had been sending students of his introductory course in Ethics to interview slum landlords in Houston and San Antonio on how they saw their business. (It turned out of course that they were very flattered at being asked, and very interested in discussing the moral dimensions undeniably attributable to their activities. Then as now.)

I think he appreciated my remembering his old lecture-room jokes when we chatted over the hedge fifteen or so years later. (The hedge became almost another lectern as the years went by.) He was exactly the same as he had been in my youth, a world-famous, white-haired old professor – and I had gone on to become successively law student, commercial lawyer and bankruptcy judge in that same period. Funnily enough, I had a feeling that he was the one who had moved on, while I was the one who had stood still.

Anselm's argument, as I've said, was something he kept reverting to all his life. He wrote one article after another – somewhat discreetly hidden in third- and fourth-rate academic journals, because they had little to do with his real subject, Semantics, and it seemed that he preferred to be known for his contributions in that sphere – to show that the whole Argument was misconceived. The historical commentators, Descartes, Leibnitz, Kant, Koyré, Findlay and all that crowd, if I remember rightly, had based their arguments on the wrong part, Anselm's *Proslogion I*. But *Proslogion I* is just a theoretical preliminary. It's in *Proslogion III* that the real Argument appears. He was very precise about that. Anyone who just goes by the propositions in the great Anselm's *Proslogion I* misses the point. Descartes did, and so did Leibnitz. But Professor Van de Rouwers and his students in the "Introductory Course on the Problems of Philosophy" didn't make that mistake. They studied the real Argument.

With those five-hundred-foot-high marble cliffs opposite us in the bend of the river, the sun vanishes over the top by three o'clock at this time of year. You'd think we were on the west side, but the river swings so abruptly to the north here that we actually get the sunsets on the other side. There's nothing to say that rivers should flow straight.

It gets dark earlier in the evenings now and we must soon be approaching the change to winter time again, but I always forget on what date it occurs. I have to switch on the light above my desk even before dinner. Am reading the newspaper; I almost never watch television, I read the news in the paper instead. I read cases after dinner – if there's anything to read: I have two competent assistants who prepare most things – while Claire sits in the comfortable chair with her novels. She has lively cultural interests. I have interests of my own.

Am sitting reading on the verandah. Still a slight smell of smoke from the charred marina. I can just about make out through the afternoon haze a couple of mobile cranes moving around over there. Clearing up, I suppose. And the sudden flashing light of a police car turning. (Several times had to get out the binoculars that I always have ready by the window overlooking the lake.) Well, the arson enquiry is under way. Nothing but horror stories in the newspapers as usual. Perhaps I'm simply noticing them more than before. I've begun to realise that cruelty has vast reserves. I'm more sensitive to it now.

Just listen to this: the owner of a Mexican funeral parlour in Houston has threatened a poor family that he won't proceed with the burial of a recently-murdered sister if they can't raise the money. When they tried offering their watches (for lack of cash), the man is reported as saying "I'm not a damned pawnbroker". Funnily enough the *Houston Post* gives his name and address. That must have involved a certain amount of discussion on the editorial floor. Whose will the responsibility be if a few displeased relatives of the dead woman come over and burn his house down? Perhaps that was what the reporter wanted? And look at this: Someone has kept a child, a nine-year-old, captive in a portable home until the boy was found half dead of pneumonia. Why do such terrible things always happen in these portable houses? They stand like boxes on rented land on the edge of cities, clothes-lines strung between them, children playing. Reservations, not for the poorest of the poor (they have no homes at all), but rather for a special kind of people, a special culture living by its own rules. What does actually go on in these peripheral settlements? How can a nine-year-old boy be kept chained to a radiator? And how can you believe that the doctor wouldn't notice when he is asked to come and treat a child who is dying of pneumonia? Does he really see only lungs?

And why chain the boy up? What motive could there be? I'm glad I'm not a criminal judge. I don't think I could handle it.

In a word, cruelty has unbelievable reserves. I'm thinking of Windy's stories. Including the latest one about the boy in Alaska. Each one of her stories is worse than the last. Stories just like the one about the boy who was chained up.

I don't think, quite honestly, that it was the existence of God that interested me so much at that time. It may be true that Jews, with certain exceptions, don't like pondering theological questions. It's regarded as rather Christian to do that. A real Jew discusses his moral duties, not the qualities of God – which strictly speaking he shouldn't give a damn about – not theology, in other words. No, it was much more the idea of something that *must* exist that was so fascinating. I've often wondered what happens about good and evil if you think along those lines. Assume for instance that there is no morality in the world we live in, none at all. Everything is permitted. Moral concepts are just anthropology, rather like table manners. OK. But let's assume then that there is an imaginary world where good and evil exist, where moral concepts are not simply to do with customs and etiquette. Why shouldn't

I be able to be as cruel as Caligula? Why should only Roman emperors have fun?

The mere possibility of imagining a morality in an imaginable world makes it of course valid in all worlds.

Because it is *imaginability* that is the point here.

I've never really forgotten the Introduction to Philosophy that I attended at University in, I think, the autumn term of 1961. That's evident from the amount I can recall with very little effort.

Van de Rouwers gave new life to old texts, as he did for instance with Anselm of Canterbury's Ontological Argument for the existence of God. I remember discussing that with a fellow-student – was it Paul, or someone else? – the entire way home from the University, and continuing from my door back to his, just because we didn't want to stop. I don't know how many times we traversed the route between Jester Dormitory and Speedway Street that beautiful late-autumn afternoon in 1961. One of those golden autumn days when everything seems to stand still and the only sound to be heard is the thrushes in the trees.

He made us see the Argument with new eyes. "A being that of necessity must exist."

And he told us about the critics, from Gaunilo to Kant: "One hundred real dollars amount to not a jot more than one hundred possible ones." An argument that was more comprehensible then, in 1961, than nowadays when everybody confounds that metaphor with their credit cards. A credit card in my pocket doesn't look at all like a hundred dollars.

My view is: The same must apply to good and evil as to Anselm's God. If they are imaginable, they must exist.

The dog. My God, the *dog*. I'd almost forgotten that story. The dog must have been burnt by now. Or is rubbish perhaps not incinerated?

As I leaf through the newspaper I can hear Claire scolding Antonia, the Colombian woman, in the kitchen. But I don't know what about. It's quite peaceful at this time of year. Not many cars from the land side of the house. In spring and summer it's the students taking the wrong turning, of course, as they seek out the little café, down by the river. There are usually various bands playing there on summer evenings. Old dusty tracks, maybe Indian paths once, where you have to pay careful attention at crossroads if you want to go the right way. There used to be a lot of visitors before, and they used to have considerable trouble finding their way. I'm not sure why, but there are fewer now.

The smell of that damned burnt marina. Will they never finish the clearing-up?

9. *The One Hundred and Fifty Articles*

IF ONLY THE AUTUMN rains would stop. There hasn't been so much rain in the autumn in living memory. Lake Travis hasn't risen so high over its banks since 1947. Dr Werbow, the former Dean from the 1960s, has just phoned to say that the yachts in Lake Travis are now moored to the boat-club roof! Which means that many of the summer cottages up there must be lying "full fathom five", as the Bard has it! Four of the five storm gates in Mansfield Dam have been opened. Our jetties won't stand a chance!

Diluvium, the Flood, in other words. A punishment from God, perhaps?

The water is rising so fast now that I can see the difference from my window, hour by hour. It's rather horrible, some boathouses and jetties are already floating past on the current. They must have opened all five floodgates up at Mansfield Dam by this stage. Claire and I are beginning to feel a bit like a couple of cockroaches trapped at the bottom of the bath when someone has turned on the tap. And Claire with her claustrophobia! There's even talk of evacuation down here by the beaches. The manager of Tom Thumb is afraid the whole shop will be swept away. What's he got to worry about? If anyone's insured, he is! And he's higher than we are! Well, I'm staying calm for the time being. The Court is closed for Thanksgiving: I've got plenty of time to follow developments. But if only the rain would stop, that incessant, heavy, pouring rain that's been going on for more than ten days.

There won't be any more major fires, anyway. Everything is

very wet, there's a constant dripping from the clumps of Spanish moss in my big old oak trees.

At last I'm beginning to get on the track of something. Whatever they say about me, they can't deny I've got a nose. A keen and sensitive nose. Like an old-fashioned English bloodhound. I sometimes pick up a scent. The Old Man wasn't allowed to teach in the final year before he died. That's probably what killed him. It's very unusual for a retired professor not to be given a little course to do after he's sixty-five. This was a world-renowned teacher who had produced pioneering work in his field. There must be something behind it. I was convinced there was! But I didn't know what.

The solution came, as always, from a quite unexpected source. The student! That little chestnut-brown girl who used to work as a cashier at Tom Thumb late in the evenings (she was always leaning forward in a delightful manner; you could see that she never wore a bra). On the way home yesterday afternoon, in the incessant rain, I suddenly saw her standing at a bus stop, very wet, with no umbrella. She was standing there in her serious slightly hunched manner, trying to protect herself as well as she could against the rain with a newspaper over her shoulders.

It's not that I'm in love with this actually rather unattractive student, it's just that certain people stick in our minds in a special way. Of course I stopped immediately and offered her a lift. Who would have expected anything else? I'm a gentleman, after all. And a Federal judge besides, which ought to reassure solitary ladies at bus stops to whom I offer lifts. She did indeed accept my offer gratefully. She filled the car with the smell of damp wool and Chanel No. 5, and almost immediately began talking about the Old Man. What had happened was that Jennifer had acquired a new boyfriend, a PhD student, and he had apparently got something sensational and quite shattering to tell her. Something that clearly sheds new light on the whole affair. It turns out that she lives in Jester, dreadful student accommodation in the totally opposite direction from my route home. So we had time to talk a little. What amazing things I learnt! I haven't got to the bottom of them yet, that much is clear.

The most remarkable thing of all is that I knew it. When I saw her standing there in the rain with her pathetic newspaper over her head and shoulders, and with the water pouring down her back – *I knew* at that very moment that she would solve the riddle of the Old Man for me.

How could I have known?

She's promised that she and her boyfriend will come to my place – it looks as if it will be for tea and cakes on Friday afternoon – so that her boyfriend can tell me himself. About what he knows.

If we still have a house left by Friday, of course. It's really horrific now, with entire trees floating past, and you can't even see the tops of my bushes on the beach any more. There's a strong current beneath the balcony of my study. I joke with Claire that it's time to plant a few trout in the water, but she's not amused. In fact she doesn't think I'm taking the situation as seriously as it merits. She feels I'm enjoying the danger too much.

At last. The water, the brown, turbulent water, has now begun to calm down a little. Maybe they've taken the opportunity to close at least some of the floodgates up at Mansfield Dam. The shoreline looks terrible: dead, grey mud, all shiny and slippery. And there's an odour of death, water and sediment!

The trees on the shoreline are fantastic. There's lake weed hanging from the branches that makes them appear to have grown long hair. And a very old bath towel. It's impossible to walk down there. The whole area is deep in mud. The stone reinforcements are still under water. I wonder how well they've held. And another question, which I'd rather not think about, is whether the house foundations have been damaged by the water in any way. I'll get our friend and handyman,

Kahn the carpenter, to come and check next week. The water's still too high at present.

Just as I'd thought all along, it turns out that this student – Jennifer Martino, Italian father and Irish mother – is very intelligent and well informed. And naturally she knew the complete story the Dean had kept from me. At first I simply didn't want to believe her, so weird and improbable did the whole affair seem. But she convinced me. She really did. Her boyfriend had got it all from a seminar he took part in the previous year. Given by a young lecturer from King's College Cambridge, in England, who obviously had his own sources. Everything about it is so utterly, so appallingly, bizarre. You could hardly have conceived anything more horrible in your wildest imaginings. *Nobody* would have been able to guess it. Nobody. The Old Man was in fact a Dutch Nazi in his youth! Of course there were many young men who were, in varying degrees of unenlightened and brutal youthful enthusiasm. But this was in another league altogether. Van de Rouwers published about one hundred and fifty obnoxiously anti-Semitic and by and large glowing articles in one of the Dutch evening newspapers that the Germans commissioned for their propaganda purposes after the Occupation. Repulsive articles, published at about the same time as Anne Frank was sitting in her attic room in Amsterdam waiting for the footsteps on the stairs. Articles about the general wickedness of the Jews, their stranglehold on finance and politics, and President Roosevelt and the American "money plutocracy", at the very same time as the trains were travelling day and night from the Dutch transit camps to Auschwitz and Dachau.

And it was obviously this exact programme that the then still young Jan van de Rouwers (later to be my teacher in Moral Philosophy) was advocating in his articles. Isolation, expulsion, extermination! He, the refined humanist, wanted to see a new order in Europe and dreamt of a racially pure Holland. I don't know what is the most horrendous aspect of this story. That he actually did it, that *had the nerve* to do it when still so young! Or that he could be so bloody stupid, so vulgar, that he chose the side of the squalid butchers. Should he not have realised that they were doomed to defeat and dishonour from the beginning, not just butchers but traitors as they were?

But worst of all, in the final analysis, is the fact that the old philosopher never even hinted by a single word that he'd done it. Yet he was something of a paradigm, an example, a teacher of morals, for so many in my generation of students.

With his incredible quiet charm, one could almost say charisma, and with the ethical conviction that seemed to radiate from him, I'm sure they would have forgiven him even that – if he had spoken truthfully. Would he not have demonstrated the *depth* of his ethical convictions if he had shown to what evil tendencies, to what destructive and satanic values he had once been committed, and that he had overcome them!

If he had told us how it had been, he would certainly have shocked us. But it is not at all improbable that he would have retained his authority, some kind of authority. If he had spoken about it he would actually have *demonstrated* his own morality.

But just keeping quiet about it all! What despicable ambivalence! And not just that, but the elegantly-assumed veneer of Dutch Resistance fighter! A man who in his youth had fought the Germans in nightly exchanges of fire in the streets of Amsterdam or across the dark waters of the canals, and who was so deeply affected by his experiences that he always refused, in a reticent but friendly manner, even to talk about them.

What detestable baseness! What smallness of mind! What a nasty *petty little* careerist to come crawling out from behind this discreet silence! If you had *spoken*, you would have been a philosopher. That's the significant point.

And then the whole archetypal refugee experience, with its various stages from Hamilton College to Harvard, from

Harvard to here, that is suddenly nothing more than the vicious immorality of an escaped war-criminal. A brutally cynical, vulgar exploitation of the sympathy that was obviously going to be displayed after the War to a refugee from impoverished Europe. How he must have covered his tracks! How hungrily he must have soaked up sympathy and compassion, only then to deceive those who proffered it! With the natural egoism of a beast of prey! (Or perhaps the repulsive self-deprecating egoism of a ghastly, dirty yellow dog scavenging from a dust-bin on the street early one winter morning?) Step by step! Going from recommendation to recommendation with ever-increasing confidence. Did he in the end believe in his own invented past?

In short, I still can't quite bring myself to believe in this. It's evident that Paul must have known about it when he wouldn't let him carry on teaching. But how could I have guessed?

What had plainly happened was that a young Dutch researcher who was at Brandeis – Brandeis of all places, a fine Jewish university – as an exchange student, had decided to compile a bibliography of Jan van de Rouwers' total output and turn the bibliography plus commentary into his doctoral thesis. He thought of course that he as a Dutchman would find it much easier to locate the earliest articles and publications. That's reasonable enough. And old Jan van de Rouwers had become something of a big name in recent years. He is trans-lated all over the world; there are whole schools of Philosophy based on his theories of Semantics, including one in Paris and several at American universities.

A comprehensive bibliography in his case was not an altogether easy task. There were not only all the books he wrote in the USA, after coming here. It would have been pretty difficult to trace the obscure early articles in minor literary journals in which he was involved when he was still at Hamilton College. And then there was an assumption, for some reason, that he might have written things before that in Holland. First fruits, practically the work of a schoolboy.

The young man sat down in the library in Amsterdam and perused microfilms from the 1940s until his eyes were bloodshot. Nothing from 1947, his final year in Holland, and nothing from 1946. The young researcher was just about to give up hope and seriously thinking of handing over his microfilm reader to someone able to make better use of it, when pure intuition led him to order some daily newspapers from the Occupation years. Soon he was snowed under Jan van de Rouwers' painful pro-German and anti-Semitic Nazi propaganda.

He could scarcely believe his own eyes. As little as I can believe my own when I now try to imagine the scene. According to Jennifer's boyfriend, the fax machines in Europe and the United States were nearly melting when the news got out. Because there was virtually an entire industry of doctoral theses, professorial treatises, articles, seminars and the like in progress about, inspired by, or in some way based on Jan van de Rouwers. Now all this activity, including a proposed conference in Vienna and another at Harvard, was suddenly threatened with cancellation. What could be done?

Was there perhaps something in the Master's own works to which one could turn for support? Some theory propounding that the person we are today bears no responsibility for the one we were yesterday? Maybe he really had such a theory? I can't recall his writings well enough. It would be good if that were the case, because otherwise it would appear that both I and many of my most trusted friends had in our youth received much inspiration and moral guidance, one could say, from a complete scoundrel. (Who, moreover, had the cheek never to admit that he was a scoundrel.)

Well. If you think about it, the whole of the public part of his philosophy was about that. All meaning gradually shifts, slides down a slope, forms a perpetual landslip. The person who spoke yesterday is not the same as the one speaking today.

Yes, my old, drowned and now dishonoured teacher! I wish there were still time to write you a letter.

But then I also have a feeling that I have to be confused and contradictory if I am to express what is happening to me myself this autumn. Something is in the process of overwhelming me. Maybe it's just my real self coming to the surface? Have I too been under water all this while? And the only – what shall I say? – spiritual adviser I have ever had turns out to be a highly dubious character, not at all what we thought him to be, but a liar and a very skilful deceiver.

So all that – your teaching to an entire generation of semanticists and literary critics and the chattering classes in general, which became a school of thought: the thesis that every text contains its own counter-text, its own negation; or that meaning *shifts*, changes and creates its own distinctions, that the mass inherent in texts is like a glacier in slow but constant motion . . . How liberating it once was to encounter such ideas, when the Old Man introduced them – in a gentle way, tailored to our undeveloped levels of maturity – in his course "Introduction to the Philosophy of Language". PHL 259, wasn't it called?

So was it all nothing but an excuse, an act of self-defence?

10. Conversations with a Pool-Cleaner

W ELL, MY DEAR OLD teacher, drowned in water and
now also buried in ignominy and confusion. I wish there
were still time to write you a letter. Strictly speaking there
is always time to write a letter, of course. One simply has to
dispel the idea that you might actually read it. Why should
you have to read all your letters? You never used to read them
before you drowned.

Winter is approaching now.

I have confused and contradictory feelings. But I have to
be disorganised and contradictory if I am to understand what
is happening to me this winter. Something is definitely overwhelming me. Or maybe it is just my real self coming to the
surface.

"If God exists, whence cometh evil? If God does not exist,
whence then the good?"

Sleeplessness, a distant relative that you have to put up with
even though you don't actually know him at all and don't know
how to entertain him. An exceptionally boring relative who
once came and settled himself in the house and just stayed on,
unasked. I imagine him as a man with a grey face and a rather
tired, reproachful expression indicating from the outset that
nothing I have to say will be interesting enough to make it
worth his while to sit and listen to me even for a second.

So I have the *pool-cleaner* instead, a silent and amiable
monster who has to hear my confessions. I always used to
wonder before why people have a swimming pool when they

live by a lake and have their own jetty and access to all that fresh water flowing from the depths above the Mansfield Dam. But most of them have probably given up on that when they can see how these damned speedboats and their water-skiers have spoilt everything. Who would risk swimming across to the other side on a June evening now, the way I've been told the people living here actually did in the past?

Anyway, I acquired my swimming pool along with the house. We've used it a lot. Especially while the children were living at home. But I still swim in it every day when I get home from work, for as long as the season permits. I like its kidney shape and I like the redwood boards around the edge, cool rather than hot to the feet in the summer, and I like it having a bottom of black tiles, not white or green. It offends the eye less on hot summer days. The leaves in the autumn are a terrible problem, of course, but the algae are even worse. It's very different now, since I bought the electric pool-cleaner. A miracle machine! It resembles a white octopus with two arms which it lazily stretches out to the sides of the pool. It caresses the bottom and sides as it moves in a pattern that seems completely random, but which always results in their being scoured absolutely clean. It's great fun to see it gliding about like that at night, assuming you have the lights on in the pool.

It takes on the appearance then of a *mythological* beast, a thing more at home *in my imagination* than in my external world. Occasionally as I sit watching it late in the evening I have the illusion that it's scraping and polishing the inside of me rather than of a swimming pool.

Claire and I have had separate bedrooms for many years. She claims that I snore unbearably nowadays. And in my bedroom I have an alarm clock which projects the time on to the ceiling in green digital figures that march relentlessly on at their silent and dreary pace. (It makes me think of some sort of exhausted *expedition* on its way through the most sterile of deserts.) When I'm suffering from insomnia – which is like water receding from wetlands in the increasing warmth of May and revealing all kinds of rocks and dark ponds – I usually project it on to the ceiling over and over again to see how much it has moved. I guess at how many minutes have passed. Sometimes it's not even one. Or it can be twenty minutes and feel like only one.

Sometimes this peculiar occupation actually sends me off to sleep again. But at others – not infrequently in fact – when I feel that I really won't be able to sleep any more that night, I put on my dressing gown and slippers and creep out quietly to the pool and sit down in one of the comfortable loungers I have there, turn on the light and set the pool-cleaner going.

Its unreal and unpredictable motion is soon under way. Demon, servant, pet? What shall I call it? Some nights, at about three o'clock, a gentle breeze wafts over the lake, bearing the scent of the cedar woods from the other side, and drifts through my oak trees. A frightened duck starts up far out across the black water.

This remarkable apparatus has become a sort of friend to me, albeit an odd one. A friend who does his job and doesn't interfere in anything. Who stays beneath the surface. But who is there at three o'clock at night when everyone else is asleep and wanting to remain undisturbed. With its extraordinary fumbling arms it pulls itself gradually along the bottom of the pool. It gropes and gropes and is seldom content with what it finds.

It has occasionally helped me with a ticklish problem. It somehow releases ideas that I would never have dared let loose in my normal state of mind. I sit by the edge of the pool in my blue dressing gown, if it's spring or autumn, as protection against the night wind; otherwise on warm, humid summer nights, totally naked. I watch it snaking forward down there in the clear green water, and I concentrate on it so intensely that I sometimes completely identify with it. *I* am the one moving about down there beneath the surface of the water. And when I am down there I think thoughts that I would never dare think up here on the surface. Did I say "in my normal state of mind"? It's probably true to say that this is a state of mind different from my normal.

I need these other states of mind. Without them my normal state (contradictory and confused) becomes totally unbearable. I even ask the pool-cleaner questions.

Its strength lies in the fact that it never gives stupid answers. On Thursday night, for instance, I asked it about this story of the dog. Without expecting any answer to that, either.

I speculated on how strangely easy it was. I would never have thought I could do such a thing. And least of all that it would be so simple. That cretin of a dog suddenly just lying there like another bit of rubbish in its own blood and its own limited brain matter. And it didn't seem in the least remarkable. Is it because we don't know much about ourselves? Are we perhaps not the same person from one day to the next?

I well remember, my dear old drowned and disgraced Doctor, *Doctor Aquaticus* as we should probably now be saying, how taken aback we were, how fascinated, but also in a way how rebellious we felt that time you spoke about one particular philosophy. Your own? Or someone else's? You were presumably pretty good at stealing. A philosophy in which man is literally not the same from one moment to the next. Having to choose one's self all the time, so to speak. Because we are what we are, but also simultaneously its negation, we are both. The same way that a text is always negating itself, the landslides of meanings crashing down the slopes of the world, and all the other things you used to say.

I wonder of course, in the light of all that has emerged since then, whether it might have been yourself you were talking of. It's obvious that you must have felt something of that sort. But if we are not the same from one day to the next, is everything permissible? Is everything basically – (at the base of the pool?) – permissible?

If I recall correctly, the penalty for kicking a dog to death on the street is usually a few years' imprisonment, whether it's your own or someone else's. Partly dependent on just how painful the animal's death was. I'm not a criminal-court judge, of course, but I would say two to five years. It was lucky no animal-lover was out filming with a video camera that morning. But that's not the aspect of the matter that interests or upsets me.

What about the *secret pleasure* I felt?

But aren't we absolute hypocrites as soon as we encounter situations such as this? Why shouldn't I experience the same enjoyment as any Neolithic hunter, or even as any modern deer hunter experiences every autumn? The fact that I used an edge-trimmer instead of arrows or bullets is neither here nor there. To have killed a dirty, fat, stray dog, a real dustbin hyena, in order not to have to run around picking up scraps of food from the neighbour's lawn across the road every Monday and Thursday morning, can hardly make me a Caligula or a Torquemada, can it? Not to mention Stalin and the Ukraine, that I've just been reading about in the newspaper, or Hitler and Auschwitz.

Crime and punishment.

I've never engaged in criminal law, not since I was studying Law at University and took part in a practical course where we actually had to defend a number of minor criminals. What I remember of the experience is that our clients were frightfully boring. They never uttered a single interesting word. A young man who had altered the price tags in a jeans boutique. A young Mexican who had threatened another with a knife in a gay bar. And who perpetrated the identical act again three days after I'd got him out of custody, full of youthful enthusiasm as I was. (I can remember the fleeting smile of the tired old judge; just the corner of his mouth.)

The experience probably made it easier for me to decide not to become a criminal lawyer. It also convinced me that what's called ordinary criminality is unbelievably trivial. It lacks any charm, any nuance of interest. Sometimes it even seemed to me completely devoid of evil. Except for the victims, of course.

I've always been conservative on the subject of punishment, not because I have particularly strong political views but rather from a kind of melancholy certainty that it's almost impossible to make anybody see reason.

You really do come across people from time to time who in all sincerity believe in the idea that everyone wants what is good. But that they are mistaken in the means. It's possible that the doctors in Auschwitz who experimented on little children believed they were doing good. But the point in that case of course would be that their good was not our good. It's not that I think that all punishments are meaningful. Their sense and meaning fail the moment the crimes start to be really interesting. If an eighty-year-old eccentric in a remote house in the Elgin area loses his patience one day and murders his cantankerous old wife with an axe – something which happened last winter if I recall the newspaper reports rightly – should our aim then be to prevent him from making it a habit?

The truth, of course, is that crime and punishment, good and evil, do not have much to do with one another. They are perceived as belonging to the same system, like north pole and south pole, like light and dark. But, my dear old pool-cleaner, deep inside us we know that they have hardly even heard of one another.

Two gods, each of whom has independently created the world, and who meet one night in astonishment in the midst of cosmic darkness.

The pool-cleaner just goes on persistently scrubbing the black tiles on the bottom of the pool with its white octopus tentacles, performs its restless convolutions down there in the water with its unnaturally long arms and says not a word. It sometimes gives the impression of an almost frightening purposefulness. But it does not speak.

Yes, my dear old Doctor, this is the letter you'll have to contend with down there where you live among the drowned.

The Discreet Resources of
the Afternoons

11. *The Discreet Resources of the Afternoons*

I HAVE TO GET out of the Court building in the afternoons after the hearings, just for my brain to stop churning over the human fates that have passed before me. Otherwise they would fill my head completely with an unpleasant smell reminiscent of old wardrobes.

(Mr Tagra yesterday, for example, the Hindu engineer who took out a life-assurance policy on his father a week before he went bankrupt. A father who was dying and whom his son had ruined by his appalling property speculation. Everything done with loans from the dying man, of course. And all those irate brothers and sisters testifying against him. Being a bankruptcy judge is occasionally – and that's when it's at its best – like stirring up a raging hornets' nest. With the kind of gauze mask and protective gloves that the judge's position provides. But they offer no protection against the *noise*, the loathsome buzz of avarice, panic and anger.)

I have to get out after the hearings have ended and before I start preparing the next day's work. I simply have to have a clear sky above me to stop me feeling as if I'm suffocating. Sometimes I just drive to a park and walk up and down beneath the trees for a while, and sometimes I drive around at random. I enjoy driving. The busy afternoon traffic doesn't bother me. On the contrary, it prevents me thinking too much.

I drive around as the fancy takes me. With a preference, I have to say, for parts of town that I don't normally visit. South along Congress Avenue, over the bridge and up the hills. Past smaller and smaller shops, funeral parlours and pawnbrokers at first, and then into the district where little Spanish shops sell *piñatas* for children, images of saints, bars of soap with heaven knows what special qualities, tarot cards, astrological almanacs. I love going into shops like that and chatting with the owners in my rather clumsy schoolboy-Spanish. Fragments of lives that I don't really understand but can guess at to some extent.

I like listening to one of the more "popular" talk-shows while driving, preferably the angry type where people phone in and complain about taxes and too much money going to AIDS projects – if I play classical music on the car radio I tend to feel slightly melancholy. I immerse myself momentarily in the reality of others, as it were, in order to forget my own.

The further south you go, the more strange people you see, odd-looking homeless women who walk with kind of flapping movements, with bundles on their backs or on stolen shopping trolleys. Or bearded young men with better-organised rucksacks and blanket rolls. Funny little Mexicans, as short as dwarfs, riding along the pavement on skateboards. Believe me, there are whole cultures in this city that we don't even know exist. You could easily drown in them! I've driven out like this heaps of times this autumn and sometimes felt as if I'm losing myself, so to speak. I drive for half an hour in one direction without really thinking, and suddenly I'm in a place I didn't know I could find or that I hardly know the way back from. These wanderings, or absent-minded expeditions, perhaps I should say, are a language. They express something that I obviously don't want to verbalise to myself.

I enjoy shopping centres too, that peculiar mix of black youths milling about in what is apparently complete idleness, lonely old pensioners sitting endlessly at their coffee-table, watching the young people roller-skating. A life curiously devoid of contact, which is nevertheless an attempt at social life. The *agora* of our times.

Yet it took me all of six weeks before I was suddenly

standing in that bookshop on West Campus again. This time Theresa Biancino was there. Her eyes lit up when she saw me.

"I thought I would just call in," I said. "I'm out for an afternoon drive again."

Theresa seemed not in the least surprised

"I'm looking for books on memory now," I said.

"Why? Is it a problem for you?"

"I wouldn't say that. Just an interest."

"The only thing I know we had is Jonathan Spence's book on Matteo Ricci, the Jesuit and memory expert. A fascinating book. But it was mostly about a Jesuit in China, of course. And we have *Ad Herennium* in the Loeb edition."

She sat down at one of the shelves to look. I became aware of her back. It was a strong, slender back. All the way down to her hips.

"What's this about memory, then?"

"I'm not really sure. It's not that my memory is deteriorating. Rather the reverse. I've started remembering new things."

She stood up, in that way she had, with a nervous grace, and sat on the edge of her desk.

"Anthony T. Winnicott was exploring that. My absent husband. He constructed the kind of memory palaces that Ricci wrote about. But he stopped. He was frightened. If I remember rightly, he claimed he found many things that he'd never put there. He sometimes suspected God of having placed them there. In his path. He believed in God. That was, or is, since I still don't know whether he's alive, the most original of all his original ideas."

"Well, every Baptist believes!"

"No, not like that. He believed that God really *exists*. In exactly the same way that black holes exist or variable stars exist."

"I'm not sure that I understand."

"He didn't know what sort of god it was, of course. He inclined to think that it wasn't the usual one but one that lived a bit further out."

71

"How did he know?"

"He got a kind of *sign* from him."

"I see," I said, and it struck me how often that particular expression means the opposite, its own negation.

"You haven't heard anything from him since last time?"

She shook her head.

"Not yet."

Her foot was jigging up and down in a way I now recognised. (Lithely but nervously.) I couldn't look at anything except that foot. The movement was etched in my memory. She was observing me with her big serious eyes. As if she wanted to convince herself that I really was mature enough for the test that was to come.

"Not many people here," I said.

"Not at this time of day. There's usually a crowd of students looking for second-hand course books just before six."

I unbuttoned her blouse. She let it happen. I held her breasts, small as a girl's. I kissed her neck, and it felt almost like finding my way home. I thought to myself: This is a good person. There's a sort of goodness here, I don't know what sort of goodness, but it's the first I've encountered for a very long time. In a world of wolves, here unexpectedly is this well of goodness.

Perhaps she sensed my thought. Without a word she drew me into an inner room, small and stuffy with a warm smell of paper and computers and the glue in the bindings of the account books, so cramped with its computer and desk that I wondered at first how I was going to manage to lie down with her there. "Lie" was hardly the right word. We sat among the accounts on the desk, or rather she sat there and I climbed in between her thighs. She wasn't interested in playing, like a teenager. No slow plucking at hooks and elastic. She wanted me. With all her various lips. Which were all equally hungry, equally desirous.

We knocked quite a lot of things off the table, heavyish objects thudded on to the carpet as we became more and more ardent. She's swallowing me up, I thought, she's really swallowing me up. Her insides had a strange mobility, she moved me around inside her as if she wanted to feel my by this stage very aroused penis in every part of her vagina. She had many different aromas, each merging into another.

She really is swallowing me up, I thought.

On occasions such as this – I usually call it "friendliness towards strangers", after the Latin expression *aliena misericordia* – it's normally difficult to think of anything to say. Not this time. She disappeared out to the lavatory and rearranged her clothing. I tried to do likewise, as well as I could. She came back and kissed me long and hard on the mouth. And when she spoke now, for the first time in what seemed an eternity, but may have been just half an hour, or possibly forty minutes (all time had come to a standstill and lay in a pile at my feet along with much else that had fallen off the desk), what she said, with an admirable leap of thought, was:

"It's not that he's mad. But he's been thinking a lot over the last few years. It's something he's been trying to get to the bottom of. It stops him doing almost anything else. The only people I've known like that were a few computer freaks I met in the Seventies. They had that strange distracted look in their eyes too. Right up until they'd solved the problem they were working on. But he'll never solve his, because it's too difficult. Much too difficult. He has embarked on the impossible.

"You see, he was completely unprepared for any of it. He'd never believed that there was a benevolent power in the world. But this power that he encountered, and that he didn't know the identity of, wished him well. He was absolutely certain of that. That was the only thing he was certain about. And so it couldn't possibly be the same power that had created the world. Oh, I can't explain it. Everything was so damned strange. Perhaps I can try to explain it another time? Are you coming back again?"

"Yes, I'll be coming back. If you're still here then."

"Why shouldn't I still be here?"

"I don't know. Everything around me lately has begun to be unpredictable."

12. *Clause 11 Rescheduling*

US Bankruptcy Judge Erwin Caldwell
2 West River Circle
Austin TX 78704

Dr Paul Chapman
Dean of the College of Liberal Arts
West Mall Building
The University of Texas at Austin
Austin TX 78712

PRIVATE   12 November 1992

My dear friend Paul,

I think I sent you a letter some time around the beginning
of October. You haven't replied, but it wasn't really that
important. Just a little greeting from a mostly hectic daily life.
Mainly to let you know how I'm getting on, and perhaps to
hear something from you too. We haven't seen each other
since the last meeting of that alumni committee. I've found
it unusually difficult to get over there this autumn, for some
reason. What else can I tell you? I've got a strange case up
before me now. Well, no, it's a very ordinary case, about a
Clause 11 debt rescheduling, you could say a hopelessly unre-
alistic rescheduling plan. But one of the parties is rather
peculiar. (The other party is a bank.) He lives some way south
of Austin, in a ranch that borders on Route 35, and I don't
think I'm guilty of any great indiscretion if I mention that
he has a German name. He hasn't paid the interest on his

ranch – surprisingly large sums – for a long time. It's apparently one with quite extensive land and a few small dilapidated buildings in the middle. Not much equity value at the moment. And the loan was taken out a good few years ago. Now he's been forced into liquidation by the bank. To my mind it's just a question of sorting out the priorities and classifications. He obviously wants Clause 11, and the bank wants liquidation, Clause 7.

The other major creditor is the man's mentally deficient brother, whom he must have been systematically cheating. This brother's affairs are formally handled by the bank, which is thus a competing claimant.

That much is pure routine. But the man can't come up with a credible debt-rescheduling plan.

Do you know why?

Because every single day there's a risk that he'll end up in a Federal jail, for unlawfully trading in arms and subversive activities! He has apparently had some kind of *camp* out there, for preserving the Aryan race in the USA. We're dealing with white supremacists. According to police reports, they've even been engaging in target practice, firing mortars on the property, would you believe. There are craters everywhere, but the weapons have been impounded now. And swastika flags and black-painted motorcycles! And this has been going on for years!

The bank's B-team – you know, the rather unsophisticated types they put on the job of collecting their really impossible debts – went out there a few times to discuss things with them. But it seems he just set the Alsatians on them every time. So I was a bit apprehensive when I had to meet him on the day the case came to Court.

I don't know whether Deans ever visit bankruptcy courts. Perhaps they should. You probably remember our mutual old Philosophy teacher Jan van de Rouwers regularly sending his Ethics students out to interview slum landlords in Houston in the early Sixties? The Bankruptcy Court one Tuesday morning, that's the place for a philosopher. A real philosopher. Packed with people up to the windowsills. Scarred old bankruptcy foxes, lawyers of every description. Farmers with callused hands, small pale couples with far too many screaming babes-in-arms to hear when their case is called. Administrators dealing with a dozen bankruptcies in the same morning, recklessly negligent of the creditors' interests. Silver-haired gentlemen with magnificent mansions hoping to be able to retain their horses. Savings-bank directors who have swindled small savers out of hundreds of millions, and carpenters who have tried to build kitchens too much on the cheap and don't really understand what has happened to them. A bizarre mix of the humble and the clever. Smells of unchanged nappies, rotten wood, sweat, and the indescribably pungent odour of the judge's, that is my own, half-dried-up inkwell. I've always thought it very strange that in this ugly and over-populated room millions, multiple millions, can be won and lost. But they can.

The man was markedly calm, a pallid little person of about the same height as myself but perhaps ten years older. He looked more like a typical carpenter with antiquated wire-rimmed spectacles on his nose and a rather battered cigarillo in the corner of his mouth throughout the case. If I remember rightly he had a squint. An ungainly little man. But nothing threatening about him, no sign of evil, devilry or general destructiveness. Was it simply a concocted story about him setting the dogs on the bank people? Was this what a racist and potential mass-murderer looked like? Was this really a future *Standartenführer* in Travis County? Who would send us all to *camps* if he and his like succeeded in coming to power? And if he knew our family background somewhat better?

He looked at me very searchingly and intently, it has to be said, and he answered my questions very politely, though somewhat hesitantly. When he heard he was unlikely to be allowed any debt rescheduling in view of the probable outcome of the criminal trial, he just shook his head sorrowfully.

You see what I mean? – he was just as docile and respectful as bankrupt carpenters tend to be. You could say that he was a quintessential carpenter-type. Isn't it strange? This man wouldn't hesitate to annihilate many of us en masse if he succeeded in his aims!

To tell the truth, I can't deny I felt some disquiet when I pronounced judgement. People don't often think of me as Jewish, because I don't have a Jewish name. How would this white supremacist and future *Standartenführer* have reacted if he'd known?

So, why the devil am I telling you all this? Quite honestly, I've forgotten how I got on to it. Perhaps to say something about the differences between the life you have chosen and mine. (I can so easily imagine you in the Dean's spacious and elegant study, bookshelves and Piranesi engravings on the walls, the fountain playing outside your large windows, and delightful young bodies lying on the emerald-green grass; not a paper on the desk, because your assistants bring in every individual document the moment it's required; all the talk about education and young people's upbringing and responsibilities. Is it an illusory world you live in, something that has grown from rhetorical custom and tradition, where speaking exists for its own sake? But oh, how easily could it not be said that my world too is illusory?)

What I wanted to say was that evil does not directly announce to us that it is evil. We have to find out for ourselves. It is not, for example, like crime films on television. In fact I also wanted to say that I'm still waiting for an answer to the question in my last letter. I promise to treat matters with total discretion; I'm asking just to satisfy my own curiosity. Could you regard me as a sort of *amicus curiae* in this respect? You know I can be as discreet as a Swiss private bank when necessary.

Forgive my persistence!

Your old friend

Erwin

13. The Tale of a Dog

US Bankruptcy Judge Erwin Caldwell
2 West River Circle
Austin TX 78704

Dr Paul Chapman
Dean of the College of Liberal Arts
West Mall Building
The University of Texas at Austin
Austin TX 78712

PRIVATE   18 November 1992

My dear Paul,

That was a quick response. And of course I respect your answer. Though it was hardly what I'd call satisfying. It's perfectly understandable that the decision on whether he should continue teaching was a matter between you and the Old Man. No one would question that. And I have to concede it. A Dean shouldn't have to answer for all his personnel decisions to old friends and acquaintances. OK. Personnel decisions in the Arts Faculty are taken by the Provost and the Dean, at best after consultation with colleagues in the relevant departments, but hardly with the local bankruptcy judge. If everybody minded their own business, the world would go round a deal faster. I know that.

But scarcely have you said that before you contradict your resolve to keep this story from me, by giving a very clear hint that there is some kind of dark secret behind your decision, and that I would only be saddened and very disappointed if you put me in the picture.

Well, if there's one thing I've learnt from being a judge, it's that writing too much is a mistake. If you have a good argument for something, you can weaken your case by adding another to the first.

I don't really understand what sort of facts could upset or disappoint me. I merely wondered why you removed a retired professor from the courses that obviously meant a lot to him as the last thing that gave significance to his life. But if you say that you had good reasons and that it would only distress me to hear them, I suppose I have to accept it.

Actually, I'm not as easy to shock as you may believe. The great Wheel of Fortune of the fraudulent savings banks has now finally come to a halt, and some incredibly murky dealings have come to light. I could tell you a thing or two. Then you'd see that I'm not quite so easily shocked as you think. I could tell you about enormous loans to the friends of directors, about private yachts for the heads of provincial banks in Lubbock and Fredricksburg, and above all the systematic plundering of whole chains of savings banks with the money going into junk bonds in New York. Suicides and strange disappearances, multi-millionaires who overnight suddenly can't afford to pay the gas bill. Yes, there are lots of odd things happening. Easily shocked, me? I fear that compared with me even your troublesome and irascible Provost would seem like a sensitive creature from an Italian opera.

What do you think? I've recently killed a dog, practically with my bare hands! Just imagine! But it's done now.

A big fat repulsive dog that used to come at about four o'clock every morning and drag out the complete contents of my dustbins over my neighbour's neat lawn. I don't usually get so beside myself with rage, but that morning something snapped (it was the very morning the marina burnt up, by the way). I would never have managed to kill him if he hadn't entangled himself in my neighbour's boat trailer at the last minute.

Blood on my hands, as they say. Ugh, I was going to have a shower anyway. Am I a cruel person? Of course not! I think I'm absolutely ordinary. I think any absolutely ordinary person – in the right circumstances – would have been capable of doing what I did.

I can assure you that a visit to an absolutely normal bankruptcy court on an ordinary Thursday morning would be enough to convince anybody that there is more baseness, more vindictiveness, more petty-mindedness and blind destructiveness in an ordinary grocer than philosophers have ever dreamt of.

Cruelty has it own reserves, you might say.

With all good wishes and apologies for the trouble.

Your old friend

Erwin

14. Amicus Curiae

US Bankruptcy Judge Erwin Caldwell
2 West River Circle
Austin TX 78704

Dr Paul Chapman
Dean of the College of Liberal Arts
West Mall Building
The University of Texas at Austin
Austin TX 78712

PRIVATE AND CONFIDENTIAL   23 November 1992

My dear Paul
(*Amicus Curiae*, indeed!)

It was funny that you reacted so fast to my latest letter. Not only fast, but with surprising emotion, I would say. How embarrassing that you remembered we used to torture mice when we were at Anderson High School. I must have completely suppressed that. There are still a number of things I don't understand. The principal one is when you say that I obviously knew more about the Old Man than you'd thought.

And his time in Holland! *What the devil do you mean?* I know nothing about his time in Holland, except that he was in some kind of Resistance movement against the Germans there, before he came here. That's all I know. There's nothing in my letter about the Old Man himself, I was simply curious to know why he wasn't allowed to carry on teaching at the end as he'd been used to doing. I really liked him, and his

THE TALE OF A DOG

Philosophy courses meant a lot to me at the time. He was so firmly convinced about something that I had come to view with the greatest scepticism: the existence of moral values, independent of our own dubious existence and not least God's, that he was so certain of and saw manifested in Anselm's Ontological Argument – in *his own* version of the Ontological Argument, one should perhaps add.

The only connection between the Old Man and the dog was that they died on the same day.

No, that's not quite true. If the Old Man was right, there is a God who sees what we do to dogs. (The corollary, it could be pointed out, is that we then see what He does to human beings.) It was comforting to hear that you think there are people who do worse things than killing dogs, like Hitler and Stalin. I've just been reading a review of Robert Conquest's book about the Ukraine. It's probable that Stalin murdered more people there by starvation than Hitler murdered a decade later by gas! *This world is incomprehensible unless we assume that it's some kind of prison!*

What if the Gnostics were right?

Thanks anyway for your cordial and speedy response.

Yours

Erwin

15. In the Shade of the Royal Forest

US Bankruptcy Judge Erwin Caldwell
2 West River Circle
Austin TX 78704

Dr Paul Chapman
Dean of the College of Liberal Arts
West Mall Building
The University of Texas at Austin
Austin TX 78712

PRIVATE AND STRICTLY CONFIDENTIAL

25 November 1992

My dear Paul,

I fully expect you to be surprised to hear from me again so soon. But strange things do happen, so it's best never to be surprised in this world. Being *surprised* is an unproductive state as a rule, isn't it? No answer required. I would just like to tell you something you may find of interest, a new angle on the affair, you could say:

There's one matter relating to the German Nazis that I've been pondering a lot. Since a minority of German citizens, mainly Jews but also a few other categories, were obviously treated as animals – or "worse than animals" – during the Nazi period, we have to ask ourselves how animals were actually treated. Were there Nazi animal-protection laws? The answer is yes. Germany introduced new animal-protection laws on 24 November 1933. It was the anniversary yesterday, but I don't know whether that's why I'm writing about it. It's just

83

that this is exactly the kind of history that philosophers never take into account when they try to understand the world. But really and truly it's precisely the kind they ought to take an interest in. Facts about people. Not speculations. The law of 24 November 1933 was very strict. If I had killed a stray dog at my dustbins in Berlin in 1940, I would have had a fine or imprisonment, while at the same time others went unpunished for sending untold numbers of helpless people in trains to a cruel, industrialised death.

Since it's rather late in the year, I have no temporary summer assistants still around, and anyway it would never occur to me to use my own assistants for what I have to admit is purely personal research. But I had the inspired idea of ringing up Tom Hesselmann. Do your remember Tom? The eternal PhD student? Ended up as a librarian in the Law Library? A big, friendly, rather shy boy? With his hair, which is grey now, worn in a ponytail at the back in the style that became so popular when it came over from England in the Sixties.

He is excellent. He's been of greater help to me in many of my cases than my own assistants. And he costs nothing. It's a university library after all. He's the purest theoretician I've ever encountered. He wouldn't survive in a lawyer's office nor in a court, because he has a tendency only to answer questions that interest him.

This time I got the answer the very next day. Unbelievable! The whole question must really have intrigued him. I explained that I wanted to know how the German Nazi State regarded the protection and mistreatment of animals, since I harboured a suspicion that the Nazis protected animals fanatically while simultaneously conducting an industrialised mass-extermination of human beings without equal. Something told me that this hypothesis must be correct.

Quite a few other librarians would probably have asked or at least silently wondered why a bankruptcy judge in Austin should want to know such things. A bankruptcy judge with his great but nevertheless extremely specialised responsibilities would hardly be likely to get involved with international law on animal protection? But not Tom.

He sounded really pleased on the telephone.

"What I've been able to establish is that we haven't got it here in the Library. For some reason we don't even have the *Reichsgesetzblatt* for 1933. A few contemporary historians have requested that, but you're the first judge who has ever asked the Library for German Nazi law. Well, someone has to be the first. I'll see what I can do."

One day later, no more, he sends over a bundle of about two hundred stencilled pages. By messenger. The texts of laws, policies, even a thesis from the Faculty of Law at Cologne, presented for a doctorate in 1938, microfilmed in Freiburg and deposited in the Library of Congress at the time of the Nuremberg trials. Could one of the eminent Nuremberg lawyers have asked himself the same question as I had, my question, my hypothesis, *Caldwell's Conjecture*?

Der Schutz des Tieres im geltenden deutschen Recht unter Berücksichtigung seiner geschichtlichen Entwicklung. Köln 1938.

Fascinating book, I must say. Did you have any idea that the oldest German hunting laws date from the Middle Ages and *Der Sachsenspiegel*? That Charlemagne designated vast uninhabited areas of forest as *Royal Forests*, where only the Emperor and his paladins were allowed to hunt?

We know hunting to have been repulsively barbaric in the early Renaissance period in Germany. The only possible impression that one can form is that everyone abhorred animals, and the more cruel, imaginative and disgusting the methods were of torturing and killing the poor beasts, the more pleasure it provided.

As well as conventional hunts, there was the *Prunkjagd*, in which huge numbers of beaters emptied a complete wood of every living thing, driving them down to the water, a river or the shore of a lake where people could easily shoot from boats or rafts at anything that moved. To prevent the peasants' dogs from entering royal land and putting up the game, a sinew of one back leg would be severed. Imagine entire villages in Saxony or Bavaria where every dog limped with one hind leg!

Then there was what was called the *Kampfjagd*, in which a huge herd of animals was driven into an enclosure; foxes, deer, wild boar, all creatures that could bite or tear or be bitten and torn were driven together and left to kill each other.

In 1795 there was a so-called *staged hunt* near Schwetzingen. Where the hell is Schwetzingen? Somewhere between Heidelberg and Frankfurt. I think. Staged hunting is distinguished from the ordinary torment of animals by its artistic ambitions; it endeavours to transform reality into art. Wild boar sows were led out in a row along a sort of walkway high above the ground. A small cariole had been hitched at the front to one of the strongest sows, with a hare seated in it and a tightly-bound fox at the rear to act as footman. And the strangest thing of all: along this walkway were twelve wooden figures of Jews and Jewesses who bowed every time the wild pigs walked over the boards.

Well, as you can imagine, my usual legal preparations suffered somewhat that evening when I took home the package that had arrived from Tom and his Law Library. To tell the truth, I very nearly overlooked some injunction papers that I was expected to produce by the next day.

It was solely because of my excellent new assistant that they went off on time. What this new breed of civil-dispute lawyer – I call them "the men in suits" since they seem to consist of nothing but suits – could well learn from experienced bankruptcy lawyers is that you never give orders to a bankruptcy judge. Not because he is a particularly self-important figure, but simply for the same reason you never give orders to your dentist. His sphere is narrow and restricted, but within it he is really the only one who knows the ropes. They got their injunction, but with just a tiny enough delay to make them nervous and put them on the right track for the future.

You get more and more of these cardboard cutouts from Washington and New York nowadays. The men in suits.

But to come to the point *at last*. The German animal-protection law of 24 November 1933, which thus was adopted only a few months after the Nazi coup had taken place, represented a marked increase in *stringency* both in the definition of the crime and in the punishment for the torture and inhumane killing of animals. The old *Reichsstrafgesetzbuch* of 15 May 1871, which in turn was based on various earlier Prussian hunting laws, was peculiar in that it only punished animal torture carried out in public.

Animals could not be *legal entities*, and therefore no criminal act against an animal was possible. The legal entity in the law of 15 May 1871 was always the observer of the maltreatment or the brutal killing, who it was assumed could be adversely affected by witnessing the suffering of an animal. So if I had killed that damned dog without being observed in Germany before November 1933, it wouldn't have been a crime. Yet from the Hitler period onwards you could get several years' imprisonment for the same thing. Because the torture of animals, which had until then been a crime against the observer who was disturbed by it, had become a crime against the State instead. And the State is always present. The State does not turn away. The icy glare of the State is directed at all animal torturers. Neat, don't you agree?

And all this at a time when other German lawyers were working hard on setting up racial-purity courts and establishing the difference between *Mischling ersten Grades* and *Mischling zweiten Grades*, a difference soon to become the difference between life and death! Baroque, isn't it? Yes, there are many other interesting things in this German law, but I shan't bore you with too much detail. And with the 1933 law, of course, a prohibition on Jewish methods of slaughter – which were regarded as exceptionally painful and cruel to animals, whereas the same procedure was not even mentioned in the older animal-protection law. Jewish butchery was probably classified under regulations governing freedom of religion in the Weimar Republic.

And much else of interest. But the most fascinating of course is that it was quite acceptable to be an ardent, sentimental and tearful supporter of dogs and other wretched beasts while at the same time legalising mass murder. A gruesome inconsistency, don't you think?

Get in touch when you have time. We could have a sandwich lunch down at Les Amis, as we said. It's pretty close to your office. But we'll have to avoid Tuesdays and Thursdays, because that's when I always have cases in Court.

The sound of distant horns echoes through the Royal Forest. If you see what I mean?

Yours

Erwin

16. An Unexpected Outcome

FINALLY, AFTER ALMOST A month, just before Christmas, I had my old friend Paul Chapman, the Dean, on the telephone. I'd given up all hope of hearing from him and was convinced that my last, rather spirited, letter had put him up in arms against me. There was a full moon that evening, I recall, and it was actually Paul who rang, not me. His excuse – as always, I have to say – was his confounded budgetary problems. (The University receives less and less money from the State. So it gets more and more money from private donations and commissions. A good Head of Physics is nowadays one who can sit comfortably at table with the major industries. But it's not so easy for Paul's cursed Faculty. Humanities people have nothing to sell. They're more buyers then sellers, as Paul is wont to say. Though in the light of recent events one might wonder.)

He had intended to phone, he had intended to answer my last letter a lot sooner, of course he had. But he hadn't quite got round to it. I suspect myself that his sudden cordiality and willingness to oblige may have had something to do with the fact that *The Statesman* had that very morning – completely without foundation I have to say – listed my name among others as a possible candidate for a vacant place on the governing board of the University. But of course I may be mistaken.

"Well, it's not all that important for me to know. I just wondered at the time, back in the autumn when it happened. I mean when it still felt as if he were somehow alive."

"What makes you think I pensioned him off?" said Paul. "Are you quite certain he didn't retire voluntarily?"

"Wasn't there something about strange articles he was supposed to have written in praise of the Germans when he was a young man in Holland? He wasn't in the Resistance as we'd always been led to believe. Did you know that? There was a mention of it in *The New York Times Book Review*. You must have seen it?"

"I did read something like that," Paul replied. "There was apparently an article in *The New York Times* about the whole sorry affair. With his name and everything on the front page. Yes, that came as rather a surprise. He was generally assumed here to be a former Resistance man. But I don't know now whether we should rely on this either. Someone will come along soon and demonstrate that his writings weren't supportive of the Germans but of the Bolsheviks. You know how things go. All this came *after* he was dead and buried. You've mixed up the chronology, if you don't mind my saying so. I forbade him to teach two years before this got into the news. And it was another matter entirely that decided me. He had suddenly started making some peculiar demands on his students."

"Really? What sort of demands? It sounds rather unlikely for such an elderly man."

"Well, no. It was more subtle than that. At the end of the spring term of 1990, just over two years ago, around 15 May, a few days after all the marks should have been in, I had a visit from a girl complaining to me that she hadn't passed in his *Moral Arguments* course – can you imagine, it was actually called that, *Moral Arguments* – despite having read all the prescribed texts and in her own opinion mastering the subject. The Old Man was asking for rather more: that the students should write essays. She was really angry because for the first time in her life she couldn't manage to work out exactly what was being required of her. Not so strange, you say? No. It probably isn't, if it's related to the course. But Van de Rouwers had started asking for something quite different: that the students should write about themselves. *Everything about themselves*. About their moral experiences. About the good and evil they had done, about moral dilemmas they had been through, about situations in which they had acted badly, willingly or unwillingly. And the poor girl who came to me hadn't been able to produce any such confessions. She said she had never experienced any moral problems. You may laugh, but I suspect there are actually lots of people just like that. I calmed her down as well as I could, promised to talk to Professor Van de Rouwers myself, and assured her that everything would be all right. With a leaden heart, because I could see what her father or mother or uncle might make of this with the help of a good lawyer. I didn't need to phone the University's lawyers to realise that there were probably three or four grounds for legal action here. Sexual harassment. Confidences received by anyone other than a lawyer or a doctor are not protected in the judicial process. What would happen if Van de Rouwers were to hear that a student had been seduced by her father? Quite simply he would be obliged to take it to court. That's the painful truth. And then the whole question of infringement of personal integrity. That's also a crime under certain circumstances, isn't it?"

"Unfortunately, yes, you're right."

"Good Lord – who hasn't honoured the most amazing confidences from his students! You only need to have reasonably good contact with a class for about a month or more, and you get to hear things about the students that they would never, I repeat *never*, dare tell their parents. It's one thing to receive confidences you haven't asked for, but *demanding* them is quite another.

"But what the hell was he playing at?" Paul continued. "I went straight over from West Mall Building to his dusty book-lined office on the fourth floor of Waggener Hall, where he could usually be found in those days, and tried to explain why this wasn't really a good idea. I didn't phone him, partly because it might have given the impression to an old man that I was acting as a boss and superior, partly because I knew that he could no longer hear very well on the telephone. He was in the habit of quietly replacing the receiver when he couldn't make out what was being said. So I went over and attempted to explain. He said he found it impossible to understand my point of view. He regarded it as a good thing to have somebody to confide in – and that coming from him, who had presumably never confessed his own baseness to a single person since setting foot on American soil at the end of the Forties! Of course I didn't know that then. I just thought there was something extremely strange about this instruction to the students to write about their personal secrets on an Ethics course. It seemed to me to be the distinctly peculiar prying of an old man, the cool detached curiosity of the elderly that could easily lead all too soon to a formal complaint against the University and appalling problems in the Faculty.

"That's how things were. And since then I've come to realise there may have been other motives. Say what you like about the Old Man, he wasn't exactly uncomplicated, that's for sure. I hope you'll soon come to one of the meetings in Town and Gown or the Arts Library Committee so that we can talk about it again. But anyway, that's how it was. More or less. It's probably an answer that hardly makes the matter any simpler. But at least you can't go on complaining that I've refused you one."

"No," I said. "But experience tells me that it's only the answers which make matters more difficult that are honest answers."

"So you're satisfied, then?"

"Yes, I'm satisfied as far as you're concerned," I replied.

Go Quietly! Don't Talk to the Flies!

17. Volleyball – The Immortal Game

WHEN CLAIRE AND I were getting ready for the Christmas party at the house of Attorney James Haddock and his wife Sybil, as it said on the invitation card – for what must have been the tenth year in unbroken succession – we wondered whether we should take coats of some sort with us. But once outside, we found the night air balmy, warm and friendly. I actually drove with the sunroof open.

It was funny that we should happen to talk about that old volleyball match. It awoke so many strange memories from my time in various law firms in the Sixties.

There were quite a lot of people at the Haddocks. Most of them in dinner-jackets. A string quartet playing Haydn's London Quartets down by the swimming pool. Not many listening, unfortunately. Very elegant. Claire and I on one of the marble benches for a while. I suspect, though, that the musicians are just students, friends of the Haddock children. The same white-gloved black bartender that you see at *all* lawyers' parties. He must have some kind of monopoly in the field, knows all the guests by name and knows without asking who wants whisky and who wants Campari. He even knows that I only take one ice cube in my bourbon. And two for my wife. (Claire drinks far more than I do.)

James Haddock is the managing partner in Haddock, Whitney & James, and he was lucky enough to attain that position around the time that senior partners still took it for granted that they should earn about three or four hundred thousand a year. The result is that his house, which is terraced down one of the most beautiful valleys on the other side of Barton Creek, looks almost as if it belongs to some smart Mafia boss in Sicily. Marble round the swimming pool, a tennis court and of course rooms which, in their somewhat artificial stylishness, show all the signs of an interior designer at work. Claire always points out, when she comes home after visits to these older and fashionable lawyers, that our house looks as if I were a university teacher. A cracked teapot, papers and books all over the place, framed exhibition posters from the Museum of Modern Art randomly adorning the corridor walls. I usually observe that it would be completely inappropriate if our house looked any different. A lawyer can give the impression of earning a lot of money. A judge should not. Poor Claire is a bit upset that our home is not as elegant, anyway. She doesn't understand real snobbishness. But it doesn't matter. Our hostess, Mrs Haddock, with several magnificent rows of pearls adorning her still remarkably youthful neck, brightens from afar when she sees us coming up the garden path. I don't think it's merely a conventional response. I have a feeling she's always liked me. She confided to me once – at a party like this – that she was a voluntary teacher of "emotionally disturbed children". I've always thought I should ask her what that expression actually conceals. Does it simply mean evil, aggressive, naughty children? Or is it children who can't communicate properly? Or maybe very silent children? In that case they wouldn't become any more loquacious by being in close proximity to such an absolute monologist as Sybil.

The rules are very clear in these circles. Not many surprises. The evening progresses according to the same ritual regardless of which family one is visiting. The only thing that's happened in my lifetime is that bridge has almost disappeared. Perhaps nobody has time for it any more. Everyone knows where everyone belongs. If by any chance you didn't know the rules, it would be pretty easy to learn them.

Politicians are recognisable by their vulgar ties, lawyers by their tasteful ones. Sinclaire, who at the moment is the firm's sole Afro-American – or, as we used to say, black – lawyer (he's specialising in immigration law if I'm not mistaken, and has so far not managed to save a single Hispanic from being deported) is the only one still wearing "matching" colours, a little touch that you only see nowadays on young car salesmen. What a child he is!

A typical feature of this environment is that people know a great deal more about one another than they would ever allow themselves to show. Or say. That's why it's all so lacking in surprises.

As the evening progresses, groups of different types of participants tend to converge in different rooms. Wives in the living room. Younger colleagues and their wives and girl-friends around the bar out on the patio. The older and more prestigious gentlemen indoors in the library. With of course a somewhat older female lawyer or two mixed in. Only there do you get to hear interesting news: of local politics, or of new scandals in the savings banks.

I belong to the prestigious category, so I sit in the senior partner's library with the politicians and a selection of the older lawyers. A lot about political problems and a lot about campaign contributions and the like, but everything just casually alluded to. After all, it's Christmas, for God's sake.

James reminded me (in an attempt to be pleasant and light-hearted, I assume) about our time together in the Sixties, when we both worked for Westminster & Minotti, a small, close-knit and rather unusual firm right in the centre of the city. It was in what was called The Gracy Title Company Building, but it was Haddock who hit upon the idea of calling it The Greasy Tile Building. It really did have an aroma of old rancid fat about it, a reek of badly maintained air-conditioning filters full of evil-smelling moulds.

"And," said James Haddock, who was in his best party humour that evening, "do you remember that there wasn't a single room with windows in the entire firm?"

"Yes, I remember," I replied. "That was a kind of architecture that was popular for a while in the Fifties. Windows were regarded as bad for the concentration. If they thought about it all. I doubt whether they did. The architecture of the Fifties."

"I remember," said James, "sitting there working for sixteen hours and not knowing whether it was dark or light outside, pouring rain or bright sunshine. I could see what season it was from the length of the shadow of my car against the cycle shed when I came out to the car park."

"You must have worked like slaves at that place."

(It was old Appeal Court Judge Archibald Reed who said that, and not entirely without irony, since he himself had been an assistant in the Supreme Court while we were toiling away on bankruptcies and debt-recovery cases at the Greasy Tile. He comes from a higher-class background, so to speak. And he probably never worked half as hard as we did. And his financial and social rewards have been significantly greater. If the Democrats were to win a presidential election he might well become Attorney General. He was formerly Haddock's most respected partner, and senior to him.)

"Yes, but at least I was fortunate enough to transfer to you and get the chance of a rest."

Haddock can be amusing sometimes.

"The firm was eventually closed down; it split down the middle, as you may recall. There are scarcely any of the others who were there still left in town, apart from Erwin and me."

"We had a number of real characters in the firm. There was an assistant lawyer who had a *cum laude* from Harvard and only stayed with us for six months. Then he went to live in a caravan in The Valley and started defending Mexican seasonal workers against their employers. The judges there were a bit shaken at first. They weren't used to such a sophisticated lawyer. And I think they were even more dumbfounded when he started demanding that some of them should be dismissed. I wonder if he's still there. Or whether they've managed to kick him upstairs to Washington."

"The last I heard was that he was still living in a caravan. What was his name? Joel? Joel Norell or something like that."

"Yes, something like that. Do you remember the big volleyball match, by the way?"

"Oh, you mean the Immortal Game! That was what led indirectly to the break-up of the firm. Yes, I won't easily forget that match. But do we really want to hear that old story this evening?"

(He looked around the room doubtfully. We now had a whole circle of respectable listeners in Haddock's dark-brown genuine English-manor-house-style oak-panelled library. I could understand Haddock's doubts about relating the story publicly. It was so bizarre and scandalous that it could probably still rekindle strong feelings in various parts of town. And when you tell such a large and mixed company as this was becoming, there was no knowing who might be listening.)

Nevertheless, I eventually stepped in, irresistibly drawn by my subject, I suppose one could say. The whole firm was going on a staff picnic in Zilker Park one Saturday. And some genius (even today no one can really be sure who) had decided that after the picnic, which was very unpretentious and bought on plastic plates from a barbecue firm – this was long before the champagne years of the early Eighties, and habits among Texan lawyers were still fairly ascetic – someone had thought that it would be fun to play volleyball afterwards. No one of course had fully realised how great the suppressed aggression actually was at Westminster & Minotti.

It began, I seem to recall, with a rather clumsy assistant lawyer, big, heavy and a good six feet – I've forgotten his name, but I remember him as tall, bearded and wearing thick-lensed glasses – taking a few sudden steps backwards and almost crushing the foot of the firm's generally detested female accountant, Miss Jones. If my memory serves me correctly, she also acted as head of personnel.

Why was she so disliked? I have no idea now. I can't even remember that. I do recall that she had to be led off the pitch hopping on one leg and angrily rejecting all attempts from the poor culprit to find her a taxi. She preferred to sit and suffer while the game was gradually resumed. Which I think she took as an even greater insult.

In volleyball the chances of injuring an opponent on the other side of the net are minimal, since it's so high that only a giant can make a direct throw. That's why it's called volley-ball, of course. But there's always a kind of competition on one's own side about who should take the ball. Especially in such spontaneously picked teams, where some people haven't played for years, perhaps not in their entire lives.

As luck would have it, three young assistant lawyers who had been at odds for a long time happened to end up on the same side. Tom, Jerry and myself. We had normally avoided one another in the corridors for the previous six months or so. Especially Tom and I. Tom had got first chair in a trial where it was completely obvious that I was the more knowledgeable one, and I was reduced to sitting on the front bench and keeping the files in order. I saw it as an indication of favouritism. And now all three of us were there on the same side. Jerry was annoying in a different way: he wrote endless academic reports instead of going to the heart of the matter; he was the type who seems never to get away from university and into his profession. For some reason he was considered intelligent. There was a kind of tittering nervousness in the air; the secretaries and summer temps who stood watching were giggling rather a lot. Perhaps we became careless. Tom, Jerry and I collided a few times in various combinations – perhaps over-eager to take balls that went an unexpectedly long way from the net – before the major impact which left Tom lying on the grass with mild concussion. I have absolutely no recollection now who it was he collided with; you really can't remember such things after so many years.

Great commotion, of course. Somebody wanted to send for an ambulance and someone else drenched him with a bottle of ice-cold fizzy drink. Tom sat up and stared around him with rather bloodshot eyes, and quickly discovered that what had been poured over him was a bottle of the stickiest orangeade there was in the hamper. Believe it or not, he jumped up and into the game again and everyone continued as if nothing had happened. It had become a sort to duty to keep going now, and to put a brave face on things.

The only difference was that the game became even more frenetic. An extremely unpopular younger partner on the other side of the net – I think his name was Hunchman and everyone called him Henchman – managed to twist his knee a few minutes later, so that we actually did have to summon an ambulance. But even then there were a few tough guys who wanted to carry on. And actually did so as soon as the ambulance had closed its doors and driven off. The whole thing had more or less become a matter of prestige. Unless my memory plays me false, the ambulance was there again a little later on to attend to two men who had headed each other.

That volleyball afternoon, to the best of my recollection now, was something of a *bloodbath*. There wasn't a single participant the next day who wasn't hobbling around in the corridors at Greasy Tile or wearing some kind of bandage. If it wasn't sprained knees and trips to hospital, it was swollen noses and black eyes. God, the number of elbows that had suddenly appeared in the world! And what was so interesting was that all the really seriously injured, the ones who had to be taken to hospital by ambulance or who had to walk with a stick for a few weeks, were the disagreeable ones, the brutal careerists, the petty and the cowardly ingratiating colleagues in the firm – in brief, the generally despised ones. I have to say that the whole thing looked afterwards like a kind of mediaeval judgement of God.

But very little was said about the affair.

Who had tripped up whom or who had struck whom was never properly established. It was regarded as a topic of conversation not be embarked upon voluntarily. But the famous volleyball match – my friends and I always called it

The Immortal Game after a renowned chess contest that was played in London in 1851 (Andersen – Kieseritsky), where the victor sacrifices both his castles in turn before suddenly winning – well, that immortal volleyball game – I'm obviously getting a bit too verbose, it's the champagne – marked the onset of Westminster & Minotti's demise.

I think it became too much for them, and six months later the firm was broken up, not into two, as would have been more normal, but into three different parts. They realised they had staff they would have taken the greatest delight in strangling or beating to death with a rusty old golf club, had they not been inhibited by legal and social constraints.

Quite simply, people discovered how little they actually liked one another.

"I certainly remember that match," said my host, James Haddock. "Especially getting knocked out. But I didn't remember our calling it The Immortal Game."

"But *I* wasn't one of the players," I hastened to assure him. "I was involved in looking after a lot of the accident cases. I was the one, if I recall, who had to keep running to the telephone all the time."

"I was brought round by you pouring a bottle of drink over me, the stickiest orangeade imaginable."

"Really," I replied. " I didn't remember it was you who was concussed. I thought it was Tom. I thought you were the one with the knee injury."

"To change the subject," said Tom Huey casually, who was also sitting there in the half-darkness of the library and whom I hadn't actually noticed before, "did you sort out that dog?"

"*What dog?*"

"I met your neighbour the other day, Glaser, or whatever his name is. The tax lawyer. He said you'd had a bit of unusual trouble with a large yellow dog who was running around dragging your rubbish out on to his lawn."

"Ah, Glaser, the tax lawyer. Yes, I know him. But I haven't got a dog."

"No. He said that you had some kind of problem with a dog who kept raiding your dustbin."

"I see. No. Well, yes, that was while ago. In the autumn. There hasn't been any trouble lately. I guess something must have happened to the dog. There's been a lot of flooding."

"H'm," said my host absent-mindedly. "Now, I'd like to introduce you to the new judge in Lockhart. Edgar B. Thomas, as you know. He's from us, of course, though he's been in Washington for a time, in the Department of Justice. He succeeds that very elderly judge, the one who had a peculiar old clerk."

James left us together immediately. I wonder how much he knew about the business with the dog. Probably only a few vague snippets.

It turned out that the new judge in Lockhart had a brother who was a professor of Psychology at Brandeis. Like all the other judges in Lockhart, this one was elected. His whole style was very much what you'd expect of a nice young Texas Democrat. Lively social interests. A bit of legal activism. (But not enough to make me angry.) We talked for a while about "the homeless". And what the word should actually mean. I think I shocked him a little at one point, but if so he hid it very well. I asked him if he'd noticed that the homeless had a strange fascination for really odd public works of art. Those utterly tasteless, idiotic and bizarre group sculptures you see in parks that seem to have appeared through some planning error. They gather around them, sleep in their shade, use them as tables. But only if the monuments are really ugly.

When he didn't exactly manifest his sympathy for that view of social problems, I asked rather tentatively whether he'd heard about his predecessor, and particularly about his strange old clerk. A rather interesting and slightly unpleasant story, I thought.

He looked at me in surprise, the new man.

18. The Elephant of Lockhart

I WAS REALLY PLEASED with Claire that evening; she did well. Much better than I did, since I probably expressed more provocative opinions about the homeless and such than I should have done. But she was fine.

There's always a risk nowadays that she'll drink a bit too much at parties. Not so much that it becomes embarrassing, but enough to give the impression of being too loquacious. It's also very obvious that she now drinks at lunchtime, and not only when she eats out with friends. But it was all right at James Haddock's Christmas party. It hurts me to see her big strong serious face growing older. It hurts me to detect the faint, subtle aroma of acetone from her body, which is the first sign of a damaged liver.

I've always loved her dearly. I feel a deep affection even for what has become her rather overweight body. It would hurt me if she got the impression in any way that I was checking or watching what she did.

But yesterday for some reason she was functioning like clockwork. She even came to fetch me and joined in the last of the conversation. She usually sticks to the tennis-playing housewives of Tarrytown on such occasions. She's never really recovered from losing her job at the University. She was the Art courses co-ordinator, and lost her post overnight when the State launched one of its cost-cutting campaigns in the mid-Eighties. For a long time she was hopeful of finding something new. But nothing ever materialised.

"What was that story about an old judge in Lockhart?" she asked in the car on the way home.

"Haven't you ever heard it?"

"I don't think so. Not from you, at any rate."

"Well, it's *not* really a story about an old *judge*. It's a story about a *clerk to the Court and his old judge*. But it's none the worse for that. You remember what the City Hall in Lockhart looks like?"

"Like a cake decoration with four towers? With a green verdigris tin roof."

"Or an antique Russian writing-desk set. I think it has five towers, by the way. A big one in the centre surrounded by four smaller ones. And the whole thing standing on an island of grass beneath some colossal oaks in the middle of a huge square, a really desolate square without a single parked car except the Sheriff's and on Court days the lawyers' BMWs and the Judge's aged Chevrolet. And smoke rising on all sides from at least three of the oldest barbecue sites in Texas. Blackened with soot, charred old shrines to meat, as tarred as Norwegian mediaeval stave churches, the wind blowing through gaping boards, heavy old oak benches, beer you have to bring in yourself over the county boundary, and the smell of smoke. There's smoke billowing everywhere in those strangely deserted streets.

"In the late Sixties, when I was still an assistant lawyer with the gentlemen at the Greasy Tile, the local savings bank in Lockhart was one of my clients. It was several decades before the great savings-banks scandal and the job was, as far as I recall, quite an easy one. It was mostly to do with loans that had become insecure in one way or another. My visits were not infrequently combined with enjoyable dinners at the home of the chairman of the board, a Mr McGregor, who I think died before the time of the savings-banks trouble. At the same time as inviting me to dinner with exquisite French wines in a large house in the centre of Lockhart (it smelt of dry rotten wood, as only big old Texan houses can; the combination of damp and warmth does something to them), Mr McGregor would never fail to mention that my firm was becoming a little too expensive for their resources, and that it would probably soon be time to look for a more modest one. It was a ritual. Or possibly he and his board thought that we Austin lawyers with our grand University and our lack of jovial sing-song southern dialect, were somewhat too precise. That it might have been more comfortable to have a local firm, who would also have been honest but not so *scrupulously* honest.

"I never found out whether McGregor was entirely on the level. He died, but had stopped being my client long before his death. Small towns like that sometimes have fairly intricate webs of favours and counter-favours, and when any collapse or failure causes a tear in the fabric some quite amazing things come to light. Shares registered in the names of others. Loans to friends on extremely generous terms. In short, bonds of interdependence and friendship that cannot be disregarded and that can lead to – what shall I say? – investigations by Federal authorities, tax audits, scandals, criminal prose-cutions? Sometimes. In actual fact, seldom. I'm sure that smoking causes cancer more often than such business leads to prosecution.

"Mostly it just leads to what for lack of a better word I can only call a 'void'. To the special silence of the Texan small town, a silence in which visitors from outside are best advised not to try to involve themselves.

"No, I'm not talking about 'death'. I'm talking about what people take with them *unexpressed* when they die.

"In big cities all the extremes are visible. Homosexuals gather in their bars. Certain districts have the reputation of being dangerous, and usually are. In small towns there is no such visibility. But, all the same, peculiarities exist. The secret ties, the invisible agreements. Crime. Unexpected and unlawful symbioses. It's just that they're dressed in normal clothing. Not that what happens is necessarily secret or unknown. People know a lot in small towns. But they save their knowledge for the moment when they may need it. Quite often they save it all their lives. And their knowledge dies with them.

"That is roughly what I mean by a 'void'.

"I occasionally used to stay the night at the local hotel after these dinners. And would sit and listen as long as I could to the grand old men of the town's banking community (white-haired, apple-cheeked, often with big black melanomas on their faces from having spent their youth in the merciless sun out in the fields or hills).

"In that great echoing villa, with its smell of slowly decaying sofas and mothballs behind the curtains, I listened again and again, for nearly ten years, to the most fascinating stories. It's only several decades later and from a somewhat different perspective that I've come to realise how trusting it was of these old men to let me, a young assistant lawyer, sit with them in their circles and hear so much about Lockhart's 'voids'.

"Lockhart was for me a sort of *further-education course*, and I have often as a bankruptcy judge had cause to be grateful for it. They would *never* have risked engaging a lawyer from Westminster & Minotti, where I started, never a firm with an *Italian* in the actual name. Anglo-Saxon names were all right. Or for that matter you could be called Larson or Nielsen. Jews were just beginning to find it easier to become partners when I came in, but amusingly enough mostly as bankruptcy specialists. No one discovered in my youth that I was a Jew, because my name doesn't give it away and I never attended a synagogue. I don't know whether it would have made any difference. I'm not of course implying that any of the gentlemen there were anti-Semitic.

"Enough of that; the story about the old Judge and his Clerk is one of the ones that McGregor first told me. I've since had more details filled in from various other sources. As the years have gone by. It's the kind of story that couldn't feature in a detective novel. It has something of the slightly stilted *rhetorical* character that only *Reality* can produce. To call something *Reality* is actually just italicising something in the flow of experience itself, saying in effect: *this is what you should take seriously.* 'Reality' is a rhetorical expression. It refuses to go away. It insists on keeping itself in order. You can forget a real book on the shelves and it will still be there when you find it. An imagined volume is not so intelligent. This also applies to many dreams, of course."

"I thought you were intending to tell the story of this Clerk of the Court?"

"Yes, yes, of course, I'm sorry. At the time his Clerk died, at the time of his, one might say, *sudden demise*, the Judge was seventy-nine years old. The Clerk, the man who died, was seventy-five. I'm not sure how long they had worked together in the old turreted Courthouse in Lockhart. It was a long time – probably twenty or thirty years.

"I know that when I first saw it the Courthouse was almost falling down. There was hardly a more decrepit building in the whole of Lockhart.

"When there was heavy rain the Court staff had to put buckets at strategic points to collect the water from the roof where it dripped from huge brown stains reminiscent of those eccentric old maps of the continents. I used to sit and stare up at them to collect my thoughts when I was there on a case sometimes.

"It was a really shabby place. I think they've been able to carry out a thorough restoration now. But since becoming a judge I've never had any reason to go there.

"The relationship between ageing judges and their clerks can become quite symbiotic over the years, especially if the judge ages faster than his clerk and starts requiring his help to make a passable attempt at holding the threads together in the trial. And when things get that bad, the clerk can have a disproportionate influence in these small, tight-knit communities. He's the one who ultimately decides what was actually said in court and what wasn't. Isn't that so?

"Everyone called this man the Elephant. Not because he was especially big; on the contrary, he was a short, thin, wiry man. No, he was called the Elephant because he went around wearing a trunk.

"In court proceedings not a single word should be lost. I don't know how much you or people in general know about how the proceedings are documented, but there are in fact only three methods. Tape recording, which is the most modern and which is nowadays to be found in the majority of courts, particularly all Federal ones. The Federal Bankruptcy Court in Austin, for instance – my Court – uses tape recorders. I would never accept anything else; but in the infancy of tape recording it was regarded as too unsafe a system. The two parties may for various reasons want to bring in their own clerks, for which I always give permission.

"A somewhat older method is shorthand, using a special kind of stenograph, a typewriter that writes in shorthand, you could say. That's what you see in court scenes in all the old black-and-white crime films. It's a very antiquated system, but the lobbyists for the clerks have so far been successful in their demands to retain it in State courts.

"And then there's an even more antiquated method, which has something rather quaint about it. The apparatus is called a stenomask. It gives the clerk an extremely grotesque appearance.

"He wears it over his face, a tight-fitting mask that comes forward in a tube that transfers the sound to a phonograph roll. The clerk repeats in a low voice everything that is said in the court. He walks around the court chamber muttering into his mask. There are just a few, very old, clerks still employing this method, mostly to be found in local courthouses. If the apparatus isn't completely worn out and the clerk doesn't mumble too much, it seems that quite a lot of what's said actually ends up on the phonograph roll. But naturally it's only the clerk who can decipher his own mutterings. And in practice he's the only one able to check his own work.

"To see one of those old clerks going to and fro in the room during the proceedings like a fateful, mumbling grey elephant is rather a unique sight.

"In Lockhart it started to become very visible and obvious to everyone that the aged Judge was simply becoming gaga, suffering severely from hardening of the arteries. He kept up all the external rituals of office quite successfully, like a shell around an ever greater emptiness within. But you could tell in various small ways that he no longer understood what was said to him. He was almost entirely dependent on the Elephant to keep the threads of the case in his mind as well as he did. He had learnt to *simulate* an overview which he no longer had. That naturally gave the Clerk, an exceptionally pallid old man with thin steel-rimmed spectacles of a kind rarely seen nowadays, very substantial power. As I've already mentioned, it was a small court: the Elephant was the *only* clerk and thus completely indispensable. The Chairman of the US Supreme Court is more dispensable than that man in Lockhart. Do you see what I mean? This power could be felt in the courtroom. Both parties, especially if they were not from the city and so had to make the most of their time, would take a remarkable amount of trouble to have good talk with the Clerk. Whereas normally he would be a person you'd seldom see lawyers talking to.

"They almost queued to be able to speak to the Elephant in the corridor. He received them with the measured dignity that would have more befitted a judge. He gave an audience, you could say, but in a fairly terse and brusque manner. Even quite complex questions drew only laconic responses.

"The whole thing was a bit like the Gnostic-Manichaean view of the world. You simply can't *reach* the Righteous Judge, because a mumbling masked fool blocks the path. You can't break through at all, you're totally unable to reach the Bar!

"Some cases were a bit odd. Not that they were obviously corrupt – there are seldom corrupt cases – but the outcome was almost without exception in favour of local interests and against the outsiders. That can of course be said for many Texas trials – remember Exxon versus Penzoil. But here it seemed to go much further. It was a period when many people in Lockhart, businessmen and farmers, had borrowed considerable sums of money from the crisis-stricken banks in Austin. The loans had become unviable as the recession in Texas gradually affected them too. Foreclosures were placed on mortgages of empty office buildings that had never had any tenants and on local farmers who had overreached themselves in the most hopeless land speculations. Questions arose about who actually owned what and who had borrowed what from whom. Not bankruptcy matters pure and simple, because they didn't have a bankruptcy court, but the whole range of unresolved and explosive conflicts that habitually precedes a bankruptcy.

"Such cases are never as crystal clear as the general public would like to believe. There are usually a few cracks in the walls, anyway. But not in the Lockhart District Court. Amazingly, no bank was ever successful. An entire year went by without a single bank ever winning in competition with another creditor. The Clerk of the Court, if he was really the person behind it, obviously had something against bankers.

"There was talk, of course. But the remarkable thing was that there were never any actual demonstrable faults in the judgements handed down in Lockhart. On the contrary, the frequent impression was of an experienced – indeed very experienced – old Judge behind the verdicts.

"Obviously a few cases went to a high court, where the judgements came out differently. But that hardly reduced the legal costs for the non-local clients. And sometimes the judgements from Lockhart stood up surprisingly well. Even in the Texas Supreme Court. Our senior partner at Greasy Tile used to say it was as if the devil himself, in the guise of a muttering, half-blind, grey elephant, had taken over the Lockhart District Court. Perhaps he was also a Manichaean?

"In some ways the Judge's absence was noticeable in the courtroom, where the old Clerk still wandered around like an anxious, mumbling, grey elephant, while the Judge himself, his eyes turning ever more rheumy and puzzled with age, put

THE TALE OF A DOG

increasingly unlikely questions to the two parties. (Questions that never ended up in the written proceedings, of course, any more than their embarrassed answers.) A kind of *void* slowly took over the room, attaching itself to the walls, pressing upon us from above. The *void* was sometimes a dog howling outside in the autumnal City Hall park, sometimes a car engine noisily revving up. The void was there all the time. And growing.

"It must have seemed incomprehensible to other occasional lawyers from the bigger non-local firms who found themselves there. If they had not, like me, been born and bred in a similar place. I knew, I think – and I mean intuitively of course – exactly what would happen at least a year in advance. Everything had coalesced in that old brown courtroom with the leaky roof, and was hovering like a shadow among the other shadows in the corner. Suddenly that autumn, as if by tacit agreement, everyone stopped talking about the subject.

"One day in January a Mexican cleaner, who had legitimate reason to be in the offices after hours and who was obviously a fine and upright wife and mother whom no one could reasonably suspect of a violent crime, found the Clerk to the Court sitting, or, more correctly, slumped, over his typewriter, an ancient Smith-Corona. In the middle of his back was one blade of a pair of very solid old-fashioned office scissors. Driven in up to the handle. Scissors like that can be as dangerous as any dagger, and these had perfectly penetrated the Clerk's portal vein. There had apparently been quite a lot of blood on the floor.

"The Coroner was called in as a matter of course. The Sheriff seems to have adopted an attitude of extreme discretion. If I remember rightly he had been away deer-hunting and only returned three days after the discovery.

"In the singularly exuberant report that I received on the telephone from my client an hour or so after the news had begun to spread, there was no suggestion of calling in the police. And after the requisite investigations the Coroner declared (I very much wonder how long he had been living in the city) that the Clerk to the Court had tragically taken his own life. He was elderly and alone, so why should he not have done so? And apart from his old boss, he had no friends. Though for that matter no one really knew whether the Judge was a friend of his either.

"Strangely enough, one might add, nobody has ever questioned that explanation of the cause of death. As you'll realise, there can hardly have been anyone who actually believed it.

"The old Judge died shortly afterwards of heart failure. Perhaps he couldn't survive without his Clerk. I haven't thought very much about who could have committed the crime. Suspicion might legitimately be directed at a thousand different people. I think that if anybody really wanted to find out who did it, they would have to get to know the town very well indeed."

19. Nancy's Return

GOOD LORD! APRIL ALREADY and summer in the air. Where has the time gone? Suddenly Nancy is here. Straight from Harvard, divorced, and her son with her, little Tom. Well, Good Lord, that was a surprise too. I don't know what to say, but I'm delighted. The little chap will be company for me.

Right in the peaceful days of late spring when all the thunderstorms come in the early afternoons and the flowers bend their water-laden blooms to rest low over the deeper green of the flower-beds, a taxi appears, gliding along by the hedges in the rain. Nancy and little Tom, now six years old. He's sleeping like a log after the lengthy flight, his head drooping and mouth open. Several small dead beetles spill out of his pocket when Claire and I try to lay him down on the sofa in the guest room. He's become quite a little man. I haven't seen him since he was six months old. Remarkable how quickly time passes.

Nancy is not my daughter. She's my wife's. I have two children by Claire, but Nancy is just hers. I met her quite late, when she was about twelve or thirteen, so I never saw her as a very young child.

Nancy is from my wife's first, unhappy and short-lived marriage on the East Coast. With the theoretical chemist Gregor Sachs, now at the University of California in Santa Barbara, a man I've never really been able to make out. He's said to be good, but not in the Nobel class. Why she should marry him and have a daughter while still at college is something I've never managed to understand, but nor have I felt the need to pry into it. I've forgiven her for it once and for all, so to speak.

So here stands this girl Nancy now, tall and pale, with the first signs of grey in her once completely black hair which is put up in a severe bun at the nape. A clever girl, whom I've never been able to fathom. There's something a little rigid about her. A tension in her long neck, furrows between her eyebrows that she's much too young to have. She's only thirty-two after all. Apparently a good lecturer in Comparative Literature and related subjects. I even once in the distant past struggled through her doctoral thesis. It was about Fernando Pessoa's relationship to Greek antiquity. I remember praising it, but also that my praise had no significance for her whatsoever. She's never really been bothered whether she saw me or not. She's always viewed me as part of the furniture. And that annoys me. Now she's both failed to get a permanent post at Harvard and failed in her marriage. Naturally there's a bit of me, a little cold point deep inside, behind the benevolent stepfather mask, that rejoices at her misfortune. She has always so obviously felt superior to me. Probably regarding me as an idiot and a bore.

How long is she thinking of staying? I gather from the lively discussions going on in the kitchen between Nancy and her mother that neither of them seems to have any clear ideas about the future, and I'm reluctant to get involved. I can't see why it should be considered such a terrible disaster not to get a permanent post at Harvard. There are so many other universities. Couldn't she join the Comparative Literature programme here at Austin? For instance?

Or why not look for an ordinary decent job? I've never been able to comprehend why everyone strives to be a university teacher. The profession is overestimated and underpaid. I've also never really been able to take seriously the flood of theses and dissertations in the humanities. Who would read them if they didn't need to in order to get a job? Isn't it fundamentally a self-perpetuating paper-industry? And wouldn't all these people, all these resources, be much better employed speeding up the literacy programme in the country's run-down inner-city slums?

There's plenty of room in the house, and having a little boy here can be a good antidote to the great heavy boredom that always descends in the summer. We may be able to borrow a canoe one day and go out on one of the smaller inlets of the river, where there aren't so many water-skiers. Or what else can I think of for him? Maybe he could start going to a nursery school so that he doesn't tie Claire down totally if he's going to be around here all the long summer afternoons. It's not a very good garden for a six-year-old.

The river is perilously close. It made me nervous when I had my own children here, especially in their early teens. And it makes me doubly nervous with a little boy like this who comes and puts his hand trustingly in mine and asks me to go down to the beach with him and show him the frightful skeletal remains of stranded boathouses and jetties. A whole houseboat floated past the other day with only its roof above the surface.

No. The river is dangerously near. I must take the boy out on my first free afternoon. Take him into town. Find a few diversions. Bowling alley, perhaps, or why not a skating rink?

There's a skating rink in North Cross Mall. It started up in the late Seventies when people in Northwest Hills had a lot of money. I've known of it ever since it was built, but I've never tried it. In fact it's a very long time since I last went skating. It must a good thirty years ago. Tomorrow afternoon Tom and I will go there and put it to the test, anyway. That's decided.

There's something totally bizarre, but at the same time very attractive, about the idea – going skating at this hot and humid time of year, with thunderstorms moving around the horizon, when we're either being lashed by sudden downpours that fill the side streets or literally collapsing in the sudden oppressive muggy heat. The skating rink, which is the centre of attention in North Cross Mall, is right in the middle of the cross formed by the four arcades of the building. The various bars and cafés, all frequented by weird half-idiotic girls and youths who don't seem to understand English when you speak to them, have their tables all around it. The old people sit there, the slightly odd poor white women, new young mothers with their babies in buggies who likewise seem to have completely free afternoons: all of them sit gazing at the ice rink.

There are actually two kinds of users: parents more or less apprehensively endeavouring to teach their children how to skate, and a type of unbelievably narcissistic teenager, girls who are slightly plump but have attractive shapely bodies and who whirl round for hours at a time, absorbed in their various pirouettes. Yes, we'll definitely go there – tomorrow, I think. The bowling alley is a bit further out. I wonder if he might not be rather afraid of it. Perhaps it's much too busy, much too noisy?

Obviously she has finally managed to get her act together and divorce. Home from Harvard, where she didn't get a permanent appointment (doesn't surprise me, nobody gets a permanent post at Harvard these days, but Nancy of course is convinced it was sexual discrimination and is already thinking of suing the University). Home to Mummy and Daddy again with her little boy. A remarkably fine, peaceful period, even agreeably peaceful in the Court, has come to an end. We'll have to see how it goes.

Sitting on the verandah facing the lake every evening after dinner for several weeks now, with a bottle of bourbon and a carafe of first-rate, pure mineral water at hand on the cane table, I have been letting my thoughts wander at will. And it has felt very good.

I've even lit the old paraffin lamp: the smells of the paraffin lamp and bourbon mixed with just a dash of water, combined with the scent of the river out there, the dark deep river on a July evening, and rotting wood from the house around me, seem to have opened doors within me that have long been closed.

(And the feeling after such a lengthy time of discovering myself again. Never really frightened, but often faintly surprised at what I find.)

20. News from Harvard Square

"**B**UT DIDN'T YOU KNOW?" says Nancy, raising her head from *The New Republic* as we sit on the verandah in the afternoon sun drinking our coffee and watching the motor-boats and water-skiers going up and down the river. "It wasn't a secret. Or was it? At least not up at Harvard Square. There had been a big article about it in a French journal. A month or so after he died. The man was a Nazi in his youth, came to the USA on some kind of exchange scholarship, and managed to pass himself off as a former Dutch patriot. For the rest of his life he taught Ethics and Semantics to others. And it worked out all right, didn't it? So there isn't really much to make a fuss about, is there?"

I don't understand why she has to be so cold. Where can she have got it from? She can't sit on a chair without looking severe. It's remarkable. Can it be something she's learnt at school or university? It's . . . a sort of injured dignity. No, arrogance. She didn't have that strange coldness at all as a little girl. I remember her, admittedly as a thin and bony child, but quite warm and good-natured; she used to come and climb up on my lap and ask me to read stories to her even when she was twelve or thirteen years old. With her strikingly pale face and very dark hair parted in the centre of her freckled forehead – like a theatre curtain – she is oddly like her mother. But a more sombre, paler version. I usually call her privately the "Princess of Denmark" nowadays. It seems appropriate, with her Danish ancestors on her mother's side and her general need to play Hamlet.

Just the way she sits there with *The New Republic* and a reproachful expression unnerves me completely. She always somehow has to put herself in a position of moral superiority. Now it's almost a question of whether it wasn't my fault that my old teacher was a Nazi sympathiser in his youth. Perhaps it was me who had a bad influence on him in the 1940s?

"People were saying there was something peculiar about him even when I was a freshman."

"Really?"

She nods and goes back to *The New Republic* as if she regarded the conversation as closed. When she came with her husband in tow, Seth Goldberg the physicist, now at Boston University, getting on for six years ago, I really thought she would soften up a bit. I approved of Goldberg, a pleasant, stubborn, rather wiry Jewish atomic physicist. Like his son, little Tom, in many ways. Inquisitive and fun to talk to. I would guess him to be a warm man. What he wanted with my wife's bony daughter is difficult to say. Other people's *intimate* relationships are the hardest imaginable things to understand.

He was, as I've said, a pleasant man, though there were some aspects of him that I found rather extreme. For instance, his opinion that after Auschwitz Jews cannot listen to Richard Wagner's music.

It's easy to point out, of course, that Wagner created operas, not Auschwitz. And good Lord, I added, nobody should be forced to listen to music that they don't like. For years I've only been listening to another German, Mozart, so it's not a problem for me. My dear son-in-law doesn't have to be exposed to Wagner in this house. If he's very strict, we can avoid Mozart too. He was also a German composer. And he wrote operas, but didn't set up any extermination camps.

"Mozart wasn't German anyway," Seth Goldberg observed. "He was Austrian, wasn't he?"

"Just like President Waldheim."

Nancy is really adept at suddenly throwing a little petrol bomb like that into the conversation.

"Of course Mozart was German," I said, and went to fetch the encyclopaedia. "At that time, when Mozart was a citizen of Salzburg, the city was subject to a Prince-Bishop who was de facto a prince of the Holy Roman Empire of the German Nation."

Nancy loves starting a quarrel when she can. That too was a quality she didn't have when she was small. From time to time as we sat over our peaceful afternoon coffee the telephone would ring. It would be about six o'clock and all sorts of unwelcome firms wanting to sell things and organisations requiring help with their charitable activities would call. I always say that I'm sorry I won't be home until later. Not Nancy, that would be altogether too peaceable for her. She embarks on fantastic rows with the salespeople on the phone. If they are offering to sell meat more cheaply and without artificial preservatives, she asks them to prove that they really can. She mercilessly exposes their self-contradictions, asks clever questions that their poor sweat-shop slaves can't possibly answer, and finally roars a triumphant "Swindlers!" before banging down the receiver. At the beginning she had Goldberg with her a couple of times a year. We met most frequently when Tom was about six months old. That was my first period of friendship with him.

Which he doesn't remember. But I remember it.

Then they disappeared almost over the horizon. Nancy became an associate professor at Harvard, which was highly regarded, and her husband was engaged on Atomic Physics research at MIT. A fine young couple. Tom was mostly cared for by maids from Mexico and Ecuador, I think, plump, friendly and rather illiterate women with dusky, bark-coloured complexions, rough hands and great maternal warmth; the same type as the women who come and clean in the house here and seldom stay long enough for me to learn their names. I know because every time the boy gets excited indoors, as for example when there's something in the fridge he desperately wants but can't reach (who taught him to go to the fridge all the time, didn't he have fixed mealtimes before he came here?) he starts speaking Spanish. A funny, rounded, *childish* Spanish. That I've never heard the like of.

It's impossible to get out of Nancy what was wrong with her husband. I suspect there was nothing wrong with him at all. Any hint of a discussion on the subject and she shakes it off with a frosty blue glint in her eye and turns to gaze out of the window at the boats. I suspect various things. Goldberg seemed far too enchanted with the little boy, far too absorbed in that world to be able to cause such an effect.

"I don't think he had any original ideas at all."

"Who?"

"Van de Rouwers. It was mostly Husserl and Heidegger in fact, with a sloppy reading of Alexandre Kojeve's Hegel lectures mixed in, of course."

"On the contrary," I say. "I think it was thoroughly original to begin his career as a Nazi propagandist in occupied Holland, come over here by trickery and deception and then live the rest of his life as an inspired teacher of morals. You know that he used to send his students of Moral Philosophy to interview slum landlords in Houston and Antonio?"

"Really?"

"Yes. I was one of the ones sent out when I had to write my dissertation."

"Well, well. I hadn't heard that. And what did you have to ask about?"

"About their moral priorities. About what they thought of earning enormous amounts of money by taking more rent from the really poor tenants who had to pay weekly than was paid by the middle classes. It's a well-known fact that the upper classes live free in most countries . . ."

"Did you get any answers?"

"Once or twice I was thrown out, but mostly I was received very politely. Many of the slum landlords with the worst reputations thought it was extremely interesting to discuss these problems. A surprising number said they'd never thought about them before, but that I had actually made them aware that there was an ethical dimension to their activities. It taught me something that I've been able to use to some extent in the Bankruptcy Court."

"You don't think there are any good people at all?"

"Well, what can I say after the story of Van de Rouwers? But obviously yes. Those who have the talent can be *professional* good people nowadays. There's actually a technical term for it in the diplomatic sphere. It's called a 'humanitarian personality'. If you manage to establish yourself as a 'humanitarian personality', you can get through a lot of borders, barbed-wire zones, which not even the most audacious journalists would be able to penetrate. Even exceptionally malevolent dictators have to treat you with some courtesy. If you're like Mother Theresa or Pierre Dunant. A specialist in starving babies or AIDS or a friend to refugees. Naturally, you have to avoid moving into a field that's already over-established. AIDS is a case in point. Then you have to be very careful not to say or do anything that could be understood as political. You would soon have your wings clipped. And you must be able to keep quiet. And there's always the risk of being taken hostage. There are groups nowadays who don't even have any respect for good people. They see only their barter value."

"Have you ever met a 'humanitarian personality'?"

"H'm. Not exactly any big names. I suspect they're greedy for power, domineering and generally unpleasant to deal with."

"Aren't you confusing *good* people with *pleasant* people? It can't really be the same thing?"

In the middle of this – I have to say rather entertaining – debate, Claire suddenly broke her silence. And said – I almost had the feeling that she'd been wanting to say it for the last half hour but had been biting her lip:

"Surely everyone must have been able to see that Van de Rouwers was odd. He had such an *amazingly* odd wife."

"What do you know about that?"

"Van de Rouwers' wife died about nine or ten years before he did. I tried to talk to her, the way one does with neighbours. The first few years, that is. Then I gave up. She was an altogether impossible person. I'm convinced that the real problem in that man's life was his wife."

"Was she American?"

"Yes, she was one of his students from Hamilton College the first year he was there. And he got the sack because of her."

"How do you know that?"

"I can't remember now. Someone I was chatting to told me. The fact was that he had a wife and children when he came to America. A wife and children who were in Mexico waiting for their entry permits. But in the mean time he seduced one of his students. And was apparently already engaged to her when his wife and children finally got their permits. I think that young Dutchman was as close to being charged with bigamy as you can get, without actually committing it, that is. They avoided a scandal at the price of his resignation."

"What happened to his first family?"

"I've no idea."

"But his second wife evidently developed into a complete weirdo?"

"Yes, or anyhow she didn't like speaking to other people. That much was obvious. Over the years she became totally silent."

"Listen, if Tom and I hurry now, we might actually have a *slight* chance of skating in North Cross Mall for an hour and still be back in time for dinner."

"Don't you think you ought to ask him?"

21. *The Skaters*

S̲O̲ ̲I̲ ̲T̲O̲O̲K̲ ̲T̲H̲E̲ little chap with me. On a skating trip. With his skates. And extra socks. And even woollen gloves that I'd recently bought for him. He doesn't like falling on the rink and getting ice crystals in his hands. There's a summer warmth in the air now in April and it feels odd to have a little boy beside you in the front seat wearing gloves with such baking heat outside. But Tom feels specially privileged if he's allowed to wear them.

He learns extremely fast. At the beginning I was afraid he would take a tumble. Horrific images of him smashing in the back of his skull. I held both his hands to start with, which nearly made me fall over. I'd forgotten that you have to tie the bootlace a couple of turns around the ankle to prevent it getting under the skate. With a sudden emergency stop as a result. Tom doesn't like being held like that. He wants to "go by myself", as he puts it. He's quite a surprising child. On our very first visit he pulled himself round the whole rink by holding on to the barrier with one hand; he sort of tottered round. On the second occasion he went off practically like an ice hockey player, skating straight across the rink in a comical half-running style. He speeded up every time he was about to slip over, almost jumping on his short little legs, so that I had enormous trouble in catching up with him. Before braking by a straight glide into the barrier on the opposite side. If only I could at least teach him to brake! Sometimes when he lost his balance he carried out a sequence of such reckless and improbable body movements that he looked like a little circus clown. (And some of the spectators who always hang about in the café above the barrier actually applauded.)

Nasty things do happen. The first time we were there we saw another young boy being led off the rink to his absolutely desperate mother, blood streaming from his mouth. She was one of those vaguely elegant mothers who prefer to sit knitting by the barrier, rather than going out on to the rink with their children. He had obviously knocked out one of his front teeth when he braked – the same way as Tom – by skating straight into the barrier. She was on the point of collapse, and the manager or owner of the rink, a genial man, became very upset, and I – of all people – took it upon myself to find the tooth. I don't know why everyone thought it so important to find it; the child was no older than Tom, so it could hardly have been anything but a milk-tooth. Holding Tom by one hand, I skated slowly round the edge of the rink, searching all the way. And of course I found the little baby-tooth, very fine and white, strangely innocent where it lay on the ice right next to a patch of blood. We, Tom and I, gave it back to the mother, wrapped in our very best handkerchief. Exactly as I'd expected, having her son's tiny white tooth just made the mother more hysterical. I've always been good at finding small items lost on the ground, perhaps because I'm in the habit of avoiding other people's eyes. Then you come across objects instead.

Tom was a bit shaken, I think. For the whole of the journey home in the car we talked about the incomprehensible: that little boys consist, as it were, of various parts.

We wondered at length about whether it might be possible to put together a complete little boy from different spare parts if he broke, and I said I wasn't sure about that, not sure that it would be as good. As the original, that is.

On our way back through the sudden heat of the afternoon and the dense rush-hour traffic, all quite a shock after the peace of the skating rink, I noticed that he was doing a lot of thinking.

People like myself really have no idea of the peculiar life that's lived in suburban shopping centres. The old pensioners who sit hour after hour, almost as if they were Turks or Greeks, in the relative security from criminals and hailstorms provided by the shopping mall, with a coffee cup in front of them, like sleepy dogs watching the few activities going on around them.

The tough youths in leather jackets, not all of them black, who seem to have nothing to do but wander round the arcades in the middle of the afternoon. Are they thieves, or young bank officials out to value potential securities? Those strange little shops and their contents: a veritable sea of bizarre objects that I at least would never dream of buying. But Tom has already lured me into several of them. We've already purchased a big alarm clock, made in somewhere like Taiwan or Korea I would guess, that looks exactly the same as the alarm clocks we used to have when I was a child. Large, round, made of brass, and with two small hammers that begin striking a brass bell at the set time. I don't know whether it will work, but Tom was happy when we bought it. He says that Rosa Pantern has one like it.

I've seen it too now. We've started watching films on Channel 16 between six and seven o'clock, lying on the sofa together in the lakeside lounge. Nancy says he watches too much television with me. He lies on my arm and really just wants to be with me. That's obviously more important than the films.

We went skating again, just a few circuits; Tom in front with the peculiar hopping, swinging style that he'd adopted the time before, and me behind, as fast as I could in an appreciably more dignified style. I did try to explain to him that in order to skate it's enough to shift your body weight from one side to the other. Tom does things that I would really have thought impossible on a skating rink, weaving in and out between the gyrating ladies until even they seem to be momentarily disconcerted, and avoiding crashing into the barrier at the last minute by practically turning in the reverse direction without braking, and chuckling with delight.

He has such a bold and determined method of pushing himself forward on his skates that all the people in the café on the east side follow his movements, laughing and applauding. But today he was suddenly bored with it. He's like me in the way enthusiasm and moodiness alternate. Now there was to be no more skating. I helped him off with his skates and wiped the blades dry with a towel we'd brought with us. He'd seen the skating divas doing it that way. He usually had a hamburger and a Coca-Cola in the rinkside café, but since it was so close to dinner time on this occasion I decided a Coca-Cola would be enough. For Tom and myself. A hamburger would just spoil our appetites and make his mother angry.

That was a mistake, of course. His little eyes quickly filled with tears and he cried so much that it began to be irritating. The strangely shapeless mothers sitting round the rink knitting all day looked up with sympathetic glances. And the old pensioners grinned at me openly. Perhaps to show *fellow-feeling* because of my also having a grandchild. And suddenly I'm on my own by the side of a small boy who a moment before was with me. I am I and he is something entirely different: a sobbing, crying, whining *problem* that doesn't understand why he can't have a hamburger.

Traitor that I am, I take him in my arms. It's not very easy to carry him because I have the skates hanging round my neck too. I'm really starting to get annoyed now, as well as sweaty and weighed down by the child. I sincerely hope I'm not seen by anyone I know. I have a vague memory of a pet shop by one of the exits to the mall. I'm sure that goldfish and hamsters and maybe tortoises and snakes will put him in a better humour.

These damned shopping centres have been built in the form of a cross since the Sixties – this one is even called North Cross Mall – and so are abominably symmetrical. Having walked round the entire skating rink with the boy on my shoulders and the skates cutting into my neck (because his small fat legs are pressing them in and half-throttling me), I discover of course that I'm on the south side instead of the north and have thus come as far away from the pet shop as it's possible to be.

Another attempt, round the other side of the rink – if there's anyone here who knows me, I can hardly avoid being seen – and the boy still screaming as if he were some kind of burglar alarm. No sooner have I circumnavigated the barrier for the second time, the child just as awkwardly on my shoulders, than I meet an old man, a disreputable-looking man, probably a pensioner, wearing a suit, albeit a rather scruffy one. I can't escape; he's already recognised me, and is hellbent on talking to me. He must be one of those who sit there all day boring themselves to death. Retired. Watching the skating rink. And watching the girls doing pirouettes with their elegantly exposed thighs. And musing on God knows what.

The most difficult aspect of meeting people like this is that you might have come across them in Court. You might for them be the representation of fate. You might have crushed their worst enemy in a bankruptcy case and therefore appear as Justice personified. Or you might have crushed them themselves, so you appear as a demon. In neither instance do you want to talk to them.

"Good day to you, isn't it Judge Caldwell? With your little grandson, I see?"

I nod, hardly having enough wind to compete with the boy's incessant screaming.

"A bit tired and miserable? Too much skating? He hasn't hurt himself, has he?"

I shake my head in exhaustion. At the sight of a stranger the boy goes quiet, of course. Whether from curiosity or paralysed with fear, I don't know, because I can't see his face. I should now go straight to the damned pet shop, but I just stand there looking foolish.

"Yes, it's been a long time since we met."

I continue nodding.

"I don't know whether you remember it, Judge Caldwell, it was in Lockhart in the early Eighties."

"Yes," I manage to get out. (As the child presses his small fat thighs even harder against my neck muscles.)

"Yes, it was a curious affair about that Clerk, wasn't it? It was never really sorted out. Or was it?"

"Wasn't it?"

"I was at the bank, an accountant in the savings bank at the time. And we were dragged into it, one way and another."

"Really?"

"Yes, we were taken over afterwards by a Federal concern. FDIC."

"Yes, I heard that. But I had nothing to do with it."

I bite my lip. I have no reason to defend myself to this old rogue, whoever he is. But it's interesting to hear that the demise of the Clerk had something to do with the collapse of the savings bank. There would probably be a few people quite interested in hearing that story. I'm not so interested myself any longer.

"I'm sure it was someone from the bank who did it," said the pensioner. "I was working there when it all happened," he went on, with the insistence of someone who knows himself to be important. "I know they wanted to get rid of him."

"Of whom?"

"Of the Elephant, of course."

"The old Judge is dead too now," I say in an effort to divert the conversation in a less controversial direction.

"Yes, he didn't live long afterwards."

"Well, I think this little chap is getting impatient. I was taking him to the pet shop. Nice to meet you."

"Yes. I won't take up any more of your time. As you say, nice to meet. Terrible thing about the dog, by the way."

We had got right inside the pet shop, where Tom was completely happy again, recovered from his disappointment and in the middle of trying to lift a white rabbit with red eyes out of its cage, when it hit me that there had been something odd about that old man. Then my mind shot back like a spring in a mousetrap! What could he know about the dog? And which dog? The one I unpremeditatedly battered to death one morning last autumn? Or *the other one?*

(I don't know what I mean by "the other one". It just came into my head that there's *another one.*)

22. *Pet Shop: The Tortoise*

T HERE WERE ANIMALS THERE, naturally, since the whole of this story is teeming with animals, whether I want it or not.

We inspected every imaginable animal, in cages, in aquariums, in vivariums, from white rabbits to veil-tailed goldfish. It was a substantial zoological business full of children and parents of all ages, and Tom, who thought that everything was equally marvellous, went from one aquarium to the next, from cage to cage. There were endearing little puppies, tortoises, cats, big stupid parrots. There was even some kind of snake, apparently fed at intervals with white mice.

Tom seemed to take it as matter of course.

"They eat mice," was all he said. "That's what they do. If they don't get their mice, they fall ill and die."

We talked about how many strange creatures there are in this world, and whether they could all have been created by the same God. Little Tom is very interested in God, whom he says he's heard about on television. Needless to say, it would never occur to his atheistic mother to tell him stories like that. And the boy – who was left alone for entire afternoons in Cambridge in front of the television set with an Ecuadorian childminder who spoke no English – has begun watching all the weird channels and programmes that are not intended for him. Science fiction, outlandish preachers and sectarians: what curious slums, undercurrents and oddities there are on the higher numbers in the cable television menu! He had quite

a detailed discussion with me the other day about the First
World War, which he'd evidently been studying in a documentary series. He couldn't understand what it was really
about. I told him that I'd never been able to understand what
it was actually about, either. And now he was asking the same
question as William Blake in his poem on the Tiger: can the
same God who created the Tiger also have created snakes,
lizards and tortoises?

The discussion was so enjoyable in fact that I forgot the
reminder about the dog. Tom wondered whether different
competing gods could have created the world, with the various
animal species as their individual memorials. (And I think
I added: and bequeathing us different laws of nature too.)
It's quite an amusing idea that a very old god, who withdrew
a very long time ago, left us gravity. The power of gravity
permeates the world in a grey and invisible and strangely
unmodern way. Whereas electromagnetic fields, discovered by
Maxwell and others, represent an altogether different *style*.
Foolish physicists, with Einstein in the lead, who are damned
certain there's only one God, rack their brains with the
impossible task of reconciling these various forces. But they
can't be reconciled, that's the simple truth of course. They
have such different origins, such totally disparate aims, that
they obviously belong to completely different worlds.

If each of the competing gods has his own set of natural
laws, we could perhaps assume that each god has his own
moral laws. That must be it! In one system of ethics it's the
reptiles who are right, and in the other it's the mice. In one
system it's right to beat stray dogs until their bodies go limp
and compliant, and in another god's system it's wrong, utterly
wrong. We can assume that for one god it's right that animals
and African smallholders starve to death and are left lying in
clouds of flies on the cracked earth with cyclical regularity,
while for another it's an abomination. What normally mas-
querades as philosophy is little more than a refusal to turn our
attention to identifying the true problems.

I think we must have been in the shop for at least an hour. I, the striking, well-groomed white-haired man in the pin-striped suit, and Tom, the handsome little boy in a T-shirt with a cat on it, and short blue trousers, aroused quite a lot of interest. From time to time one of the assistants would approach, mostly delightful young girls who even had a special kind of uniform. And in equally friendly fashion I waved them away. We were still looking.

We shouldn't spend too long searching, I tried to explain to Tom. In the end there won't be much left. The more you exhaust yourself in the search, the more unimaginative your desires become. But that was wasted on him.

He's only six, after all. He's got time.

Having been almost on the point of buying in turn three goldfish and some sort of giant Chinese catfish (which I managed to persuade him at the last minute to give up, since the creature apparently required a salt-water aquarium with a special filter unit costing several hundred dollars that I didn't have the slightest desire to pay out; besides, I don't know whether "catfish" was the correct name for the fat, strangely indolent and contemplative beast that was floating around in its tank, but I had to call it something), he started to get interested in a tame rat with a long pink tail, which in fact reminded me, with its long drooping moustache, of the Clerk to the Court in Lubbock. A really distasteful animal that Tom thought wonderful.

After all that, and much more that I can't remember, we came to a small yellowish tortoise, slow, sleepy and passive. I'm sure it was the most impersonal, boring animal in the entire collection. But that, and nothing else, was what he wanted.

We took it home in a little cardboard box with instructions on how to look after it – that shop obviously has instructions on the care of every animal (maybe even humans too) – and, to the combined horror of my wife and his mother Nancy, put it on the kitchen table, where it soon left repulsive faecal deposits, strangely yellow and viscous, with the most disgusting little worms wriggling about in them. With a very critical glare, unusual for her, my dear wife threw the whole tablecloth into the washing machine. And I could tell that she would really have liked to burn it. I can't exactly recall the outcome. But Tom was crying, and I fled to my study to pore over a long-neglected case. And the tortoise ended up in a big plastic box like those used by the post office, with a water dish and lettuce, out in the garden. Details to which I shall return.

Nancy is odd. I can't understand how she could become such a stranger to me. A kind of fundamentally discontented person who always seems to be on the way to somewhere else, who doesn't value what she already has (Tom, whom she grossly neglects and is perpetually off-loading on to others, in my opinion), and is constantly pursuing something she hasn't got (a man, I would guess, but am afraid that it may really be a female lover she wants), preoccupied with questions, movements, opinions: postmodernism, deconstructivism, feminism, the imminent collapse of the USA – which seems to me not so much the expression of a well-considered political attitude, but rather the various expressions of a destructive bitterness, a sort of destructive unacademic youth movement, an adolescent anger that's not particularly attractive in a thirty-year-old woman. On her way from husband to husband (each more distinguished than his predecessor, in a manner that has so far proved very useful for her career), from university to university, those too each grander than the last, she has managed to avoid developing a personality of her own. She is nothing but a compliant mirror of the ideas that different people around her, above all distinguished men, deposit on its surface.

Little Tom is already accustomed to a number of Daddies, who move into the various apartments where his mother lives and then move out again. After a while. After God knows what scenes, what quarrels the poor little chap is forced to witness. (We don't discuss such things, Tom and I. He doesn't speak about his life with Nancy at all. Perhaps he regards everything as completely normal. Children presumably do.) Anyway, we're all sitting talking now, Claire, Nancy and I – with Tom on my lap, where he often falls asleep as the motorboats below the windows start to switch on their navigation lights and the furrows of their wakes begin to glisten in the moonlight. I've avoided political discussions with Nancy for a long time. All she does is articulate her total lack of familiarity with the real questions. She thinks, for instance, that women's problems in the USA are one of the major vital issues. When any sane person must realise that the greatest problem is that we are in the process of totally losing control of the ethnic groups in the inner-city areas and the compulsive, third-world type of criminality that they breed. This country now represents lifestyles so far removed from one another that they can't even be described in the same language.

But she has a number of ideas that actually amuse me. One is that Americans are not living in their own time but twenty-five years ago, in a sort of late Fifties or early Sixties idyll that television constantly reproduces in its antiquated series, which hardly have anything to do with the present. Living in friendly residential neighbourhoods for the middle classes that today's middle classes can no longer afford. Well-integrated blacks, also aspiring to middle class, inhabit these fictional neighbourhoods, while the black slums of reality are bordering on the inhuman. And from time to time burst into desperate revolt.

This TV-world, according to Nancy, is gradually replacing the real one.

23. America's Most Intelligent Man

I KNEW THAT THE marina would go up in flames! I knew it in advance! Don't ask me how. But I knew.

It's rather embarrassing to admit, but I can't quite remember whether I met Mr Douglas Melvin Smith before or after the fire in the boat harbour. America's Most Intelligent Man, as I called him.

Perhaps my memory really is deteriorating. Not so much on legal matters; those have become second nature, as it were. But definitely in the personal sphere. And as I forget more and more of the past, I'm simultaneously getting more and more premonitions of the future. A fine balance! I wonder how it works. I *knew* that the marina would catch fire before it happened! Don't ask me how – it just makes me feel confused. Like a sort of vague recollection, long before the event, a fuzzy certainty that I didn't even think about very much.

Are there memories of the future? Perhaps our soul – our *psyche* – has such a complicated structure that it actually reaches out a bit beyond time? Let's assume, for the sake of argument, that someone gets increasingly forgetful while simultaneously his memory of the future becomes stronger and more distinct. What a *frightening* situation it would be if you no longer knew which *direction* you were heading in because you knew the future better than the past.

What direction *are* we heading in, anyway?

The course of events must have been roughly as follows: my old friend the Dean, Professor Paul Chapman, rang me up, and chatted about quite a few things. Then he suddenly asked whether I would be willing to join a committee of former students to help raise money for a new Art Library. My first question was something like *what the hell's wrong with the old one?* Paul came out with a whole list of explanations which I've completely forgotten now. But we knew they were just excuses. Clearly such a committee should include former students who had been successful in life, and I came into that category (even if I'm bloody bored nowadays and actually count the hours I spend in my overfilled courtroom with its smell of fear, where all the cases are beginning to seem more and more alike). Turning down a request of that nature is something you just don't do. Paul thought it would be good to have a few more lawyers there. It would impress the University President, he said. My predecessor had been on the committee, but had disappeared from it as unremarkably as he had lived.

I would never have taken up the offer if it hadn't been for my old fondness for the West Campus. Especially in the leafy darkness and dampness of June. Young people wander up and down in the narrow streets beneath the dense foliage of the massive trees late into the evening, tenderly arm in arm. Swarms of bicycles swish past through tunnels of green. Young men in short-sleeved shirts play baseball and discuss Gödel's Theorems on the same street-corner. Some drink wine high up on a balcony that's almost in the crown of an oak tree. Others look as if they're cycling around drunk on the perfume of honeysuckle and magnolia.

Good heavens – that's it! Problem solved! It was *June* last year, and thus a long time before the marina burnt up in September. It was in June that I met America's Most Intelligent Man, Mr Douglas Melvin Smith.

So, I was very pleased to go to that committee meeting for the Friends of the Art Library. It's not often I get down there, and it's all so different from the sterile part of town where I work, among court buildings and government departments in the centre of Austin. Going over to the University is almost like taking a little trip to somewhere else. A journey back, perhaps, to the past. The smell of limestone from the old Spanish-style buildings, the odour of chlorine in the lavatories, strange formulae, strange words written in chalk on blackboards that haven't yet been cleaned, everything reminds me of my youth. It all made me happy then, too.

The mixture of intellectual adventures and others, the thick black ponytail of a girl in front of me in class and Bertrand Russell's theory of descriptions on the blackboard. It was certainly an enjoyable time. Life is much duller now. Married to the same woman for thirty years, who, moreover, has short hair, and bankruptcy proceedings instead of philosophical discussions – it almost brings on feelings of longing for the green shimmer beneath the giant oaks.

It was assumed that I should be able to find my way to the New Music Building, where the committee was to meet and confirm itself in office, but I'm not so good on these new buildings from the Seventies. So having first taken – in the humid June warmth – a long and sentimental stroll to the Old Music Building, where I found only a thin, bespectacled girl in the office of the French Department who sketched out a very muddled map for me, I continued westwards, towards the West Fountain as I'd been directed. But on the way I felt greatly in need of a pee for some reason, so despite already being late enough to have to hurry, I stopped off in the shabby old lavatory in the Classics Department on the ground floor of Waggener Hall.

I've never liked public lavatories. Partly because they're usually not cleaned and have an unpleasant smell and vulgar graffiti, but also because I dislike the intimacy of standing at a urinal peeing next to others. A judge never pees by the side of lawyers and clients. He has his own separate lavatory adjacent to his office. And I hardly ever go to the airport. Neither my wife nor I like travelling. We might tour by car through the Hill Country at Easter to look at the blossom. But that's all. Otherwise we have our house, our garden and our lake, to the extent that it's not taken over by water-skiers when summer comes. In November and December we can at least pretend to ourselves that we own it.

Yes, now I remember a bit better – it was in June, long before the marina went up in smoke and the Old Man died and the dog disappeared and, in a word, everything began, that I met Mr Douglas Melvin Smith at the urinals on the ground floor of Waggener Hall. It was a quiet evening, because everybody was outdoors and it was highly unlikely there would be anyone else there.

But that was where I met America's Most Intelligent Man. I was standing there having a pee. With one eye on the time, since I didn't want to be unacceptably late for the meeting. As I was doing so – and since I'm getting older, fifty-six this year, it takes a little longer nowadays – a tall lanky man with gold-rimmed spectacles and a rather stiff strutting walk entered, obviously also with the lawful intention of having a pee. He was carrying luggage of a size that wasn't easy to put down in a public lavatory.

The man, who must have been about ten years too old to be a student, had immense trouble. Because what he had with him was a pair of those enormous leather bags that look like deformed, or what in my youth we would have called hormone-injected, briefcases. I mean the type that are meant for really big documents: drawings, architectural plans, diagrams, works of art, that kind of thing. It wasn't easy to handle them in a public lavatory, that much was clear. It was totally impractical to lean them against the wall, because they might get splashed, nor would it have been possible to put them up on the shelf above the washbasins, because they would have simply fallen down. In need of a pee, as I could reasonably assume him to be, the man was fighting a losing battle with these gigantic portfolios. I'm not in the habit of initiating conversations in public urinals, but this man was so obviously desperate for a pee, unable to cope with his belongings and generally disorientated, that I, having finished, offered to hold them for him. Normal decent straightforward helpfulness (if there's a place for anything like that in the world we live in, which I often doubt) dictates that you render assistance to a person in a situation like his.

Only with the utmost reluctance, not to say suspicion, did he entrust me with his baggage. Perhaps he was a researcher engaged on some kind of secret project? Such research does go on in universities. He might have been involved in something secret for Aerospace? Or Electrical Engineering? But if so, why would he come all the way over from East Campus to West Campus for a pee? When he'd finished I gave him back the huge portfolios. He took them with the dignity of a prince. Quite a bizarre situation, I have to say. Instead of thanking me for my help, he surprised me not a little (as we were both going out of the door with a momentary hesitation about precedence) by introducing himself with all solemnity:

"My name is Douglas Melvin Smith. I'm here to have a look round the University."

It was impossible to say anything to that.

"Splendid idea. Are you a visiting professor?"

"No. I'm here more as . . . as an intelligent observer. I'm actually the most intelligent man in the USA."

That was also rather difficult to respond to.

"No. There you're mistaken, Mr Melvin Smith. It's me who's the most intelligent man. Ask my wife!"

"I mean it in a *technical* sense. I had the highest IQ that's ever been measured in any test. I'm a member of several clubs for people with exceptionally high IQs. I'm even chairman of one, The Octophilandreans."

"Fantastic name! What does it mean?"

"That's confidential."

"And what do you do when you meet? Devise new and ever more refined tests for one another?"

"Actually, we do sometimes. But we have other activities as well. There are lots of single people among us who come to meetings mainly to meet a partner. Intelligent people are often solitary."

"Really?"

At that juncture we were on our way down the stairs to the east side ground level, which is one storey lower than the west, and I was beginning to wonder how the conversation would continue. Although I knew that the committee over in the New Music Building would notice if I came late and possibly also take it as a sign of disdain on my part, I couldn't resist prolonging the conversation a little.

"May I ask," I said, "what such an intelligent man is doing here at the University of Austin on a beautiful summer evening like this?"

Instead of replying, he opened one of his large portfolios on the stairs in front of me. The peculiar diagram that he revealed was actually very attractive. Five different concentric circles had been drawn in different inks, red, blue and so on. I can't remember in detail. And each circle was full of tiny neat writing. I leant forward to scrutinise it more carefully. It seemed as if each word stood for a general concept. Closest to the centre were the big extensive concepts such as *Time* and *Space*, and the further towards the periphery you got, the more specialised they became. I could just decipher *Restaurant*, *Space Flight* and *Coitus Interruptus* on the outer circle. If you rotated the circles the concepts could be combined in almost limitless variations; they would, as it were, start to think for themselves.

"Well, this looks exactly like Raymundus Lullus," I said. "These are the Lullean Circles."

"Pardon? What did you say?"

I had to assume that he must have heard of Raymundus Lullus and his *Ars Combinandi*, the Raymundean Art or whatever it was called.

As it happened, the Old Man was fascinated by what we might refer to as the Cabbalistic side of modern logic, the combinatory tendency, numbering with primary values in Gödel's Theorems, questions about effective calculability, the Turing machine, and – ultimately – artificial intelligence. In fact, he was among the first to talk about such things. The whole Lullean rotation of concepts, in itself no more than a Christian Cabbalism, had for him a natural affinity with current theories of proofs and models.

Wasn't Gödel's Numeration exactly the same thing as the Cabbalists were interested in? And in fact for exactly the same reasons as Kurt Gödel's. They wanted to know whether there was a mechanical, a practical and calculable method of finding the whole meaning of the Torah, in other words *God's real name*. That's what Van de Rouwers used to say.

"You don't mean you haven't heard of Raymundus Lullus, or Raymond Lully?" I asked.

As I shall explain a little later on, he gradually came to develop an extreme hatred for me. There were various reasons or explanations for that hatred. But *this*, I think, was what really caused him to loathe me.

"No, who is he?" said Mr Douglas Melvin Smith, regarding me with an expression of outright horror, as if he imagined it might be someone in Chicago or Los Angeles that he *ought* to know of. Probably a member of a competing sect of "concept people" of some kind.

"The theory, I understand, is that these circles rotate around one another, with the different combinations stimulating new ideas? It's a creativity machine."

He looked at me in total amazement, rather as if I had divulged a secret.

"How can you possibly know that?"

"My dear chap," I said. "I told you that I was the most intelligent person in the USA. Besides, you don't require much intelligence to grasp this system. It's so simple that a child could comprehend it. It's Raymond Lully, nothing more. It was even demonstrated long ago why it doesn't work. Had you been thinking of selling it to someone? As a toy for pre-school children, perhaps?"

"Not at all," he said, offended. "I'm only talking to institutions of very advanced research about this system. But what I'd like to know," Mr Douglas Melvin Smith continued, fixing me with an unusually piercing stare (he was obviously very shortsighted, which always gives the impression of a piercing gaze), "is *how you can be so familiar with my system?*"

There was something about the man that infuriated me beyond measure, without my being able to decide exactly what it was. His arrogance perhaps? His lack of knowledge? His stupid, ignorant egocentricity?

"But these are absolutely well-known things," I said. "You're just astonishingly ill-informed about basic historical facts. There's probably not a single student with any awareness of the history of ideas who isn't acquainted with this. It's part of the history of Logic. His *Ars Magna* was published in 1305 or thereabouts, if I remember rightly. I'm no expert; I'm simply quoting what I recall from my introductory course in the history of Logic."

"What did you say the author's name was?" asked Mr Douglas Melvin Smith, the macro-intelligence, sceptically.

I had a feeling I might have shaken his massive self-confidence a tiny bit.

"Raymond Lully, Ramón Lull," I answered. "Troubadour, philosopher, mystic. Spaniard, died in Majorca. Contemporary of Thomas Aquinas and Albertus Magnus. He had a sort of mystical experience, an experience of God, one could perhaps say, in 1272, and he spent the remainder of his life trying to express it. That all knowledge forms a kind of divine system, which could be seen as a whole if we could find the right key. So with Lully we go from one conceptual sphere to the next in combinations like these. But if my memory serves me correctly, there's an upward ascent from concrete concepts to the increasingly universal and abstract, and then you have to descend again step by step, back down to the concrete world. I think one of his books is actually called *Liber de Ascendi et Descendi*."

The Most Intelligent Man gazed at me with a mixture of frank admiration and equally frank detestation.

"I can only believe," he said, "that this is something I should have known about. I should have been told about it. If it's something that's been deliberately withheld from me, I'm sure it must have been done as a wilful attempt to sabotage my work."

He disappeared into the warm June night so fast that I didn't have time to drive the final nail properly into the coffin of his perverse, arrogant self-confidence.

Naturally I thought that would be the end of the story. A week or so later Paul rang me one evening and told me jocularly what happened next. As he was getting into his car, one of the last to leave the alumni meeting, he had been stopped by Professor McFarlane, who wanted to discuss the demand for multi-cultural courses. When he eventually got away from the loquacious old man, a weird figure, weighed down by enormous portfolios of some kind, had glided out of the shadows beneath the trees and started to question him about me. Paul isn't a particularly nervous type – he was a military intelligence officer in Vietnam in the early Sixties – and a person struggling with huge portfolios of papers slipping and sliding in all directions hardly represented any real threat, but he was naturally a bit taken aback. He is the Dean, after all, and used to being treated with a modicum of respect rather than being pounced on in the darkness of the night.

Mr Douglas Melvin Smith had managed, I know not how, to ferret out my name by asking various people on campus, and now he wanted to know who I was. And Paul, who is after all a polite man, but not entirely indiscreet, obviously asked him why he wanted to know.

It turned out that The Most Intelligent Man harboured a suspicion that I might possibly be a spy sent out by IBM, the CIA, FBI or IRS. (There are so many acronyms to choose from nowadays.) Commissioned to lay hands on his new, secret, and carefully patented concept-combining methods and programmes. Paul couldn't forego the pleasure of telling him that I had actually been a bankruptcy judge in the city of

Austin for many years. That seemed to placate The Most Intelligent Man, who immediately began to enquire instead if he could come along to the Philosophy Department's annual summer picnic in Zilker Park.

He'd also found that out deviously by sneaking a look at the noticeboard, probably the one on the third floor in Waggener Hall. There was no doubt that we were dealing here with a very enterprising man.

Paul had wondered why, and The Most Intelligent Man had replied that he always endeavoured to get into circles where he could meet intelligent young women. His own intelligence had somehow inhibited all his attempts to find a suitable companion, but the summer picnic of a Philosophy Department ought to be the ideal place for him.

Paul had broken off the conversation in a friendly but curt manner. He felt that as he was so fully occupied with budgets and multi-cultural programmes and other problems, he could hardly take on the task of providing outsiders with women. But he did phone the head of the Philosophy Department a little later on and discreetly ask him to warn the girls. The result was that all the pretty and intelligent young female PhD students out in Zilker Park reacted either with hysterical shrieks or with powerful feminist invective every time the unfortunate Mr Douglas Melvin Smith approached.

Three days afterwards he rang me up, impertinently enough at ten in the evening, and accused me of having ruined his life. He would get his revenge. I had not only destroyed all his chances of finding a wife among the desirable young postgraduates of the Philosophy Department, I had also made it obvious to him what a totally absurd person he fundamentally was. I had made him see himself as a ridiculous clown and insulted him to such a degree that it could only be expunged by death, either his own or mine. I laughed. That was unwise.

A month or so passed, and I was sure the man must have left town. The only one to remember him was Paul, who occasionally – for some reason – enquired if I'd heard from him. Then I suddenly learnt that he'd come to the Court asking for me! Had sent in a note to the Usher while the Court was in session, asking about the dog. I wrote on the same piece of paper – in many respects a foolish thing to do – that he should be very careful not to pester a Federal judge in the course of his duty, and that I could easily have him arrested that very day if he didn't get the hell out. The note disappeared a couple of days later. He had come and collected it.

It might be thought that this would be the end of the story; but it isn't quite.

24. The Old Lady and the Dolls

NOT ONLY IS THERE less water in the river over the last few days. There are fewer bankruptcies too. It's as if the great surge after the savings-bank crisis and the building fiasco of the Eighties had slowed down. I notice that sometimes I'm even getting home before dusk now. The cases are fewer, and less complicated. Or perhaps it's just that we've learnt how to deal with most of the possible variants in the Court by this stage? A great many feel like repeats.

No sooner have Nancy and Tom come here than things begin to happen.

In the afternoons Tom plays with a little girl called Erin, who lives a bit further down the street. Quite gentle games, that don't cause too many problems. I prefer them to play over there, at the Johnsons' house, because they have a fence along the river. You never know what might happen, and children and waterside properties aren't a very good mix at the best of times.

The younger Johnsons have a kind of nurse, Felicia. She doubtless has a lot of admirable qualities, but speaking English isn't one of them, and that probably explains what occurred. Some time in the early afternoon today, an old lady came ringing at the door and introduced herself as the mother of little Tom's grandmother. Felicia, who naturally enough hasn't a clue about little Tom's great-grandmother, my mother-in-law Judith, who died in Boston several decades ago, admitted the old lady, and she made herself comfortable and sat watching the children playing in the garden. Apparently with a slightly absent-minded look. After a while she began playing with them too, rearranging their dolls and retying the dolls' hair-ribbons, even dancing a little jig with the children. The games became increasingly lively, the children rather over-excited, as they easily do if you play games with them that are too boisterous.

When Erin's mother came home from the hairdresser's at about four o'clock, she wondered of course who the strange old lady was, dancing hand in hand with Tom and Erin in the garden. And elicited the response that it was Tom's great-grandmother. She contented herself with that news for a while; she had masses of groceries to put in the fridge, and people to phone, so she was pretty well occupied for half an hour or so.

When she looked out of the window again, she turned quite pale. To shrieks of joy from the children, the old lady was busily cutting the heads off one doll after another with em-broidery scissors she had evidently brought with her. Erin's mother rushed out, very upset, and found that Tom's great-grandmother was impossible to communicate with. Her only response was an introverted smile and a total unwillingness to stop decapitating the children's dolls.

She was working swiftly with the scissors and smiling in silent contemplation of her handiwork.

Terrified, Erin's mother – whose name, by the way, is Linda, in case that's of any interest, a big, blonde, attractive and maternal woman of German extraction – rescued the children, brought them into the kitchen and phoned Claire to tell her, in some embarrassment, about her mother's bizarre behaviour. What Linda – with some justification – was asking herself of course was when this gentle, smiling woman would have turned to decapitating the children. When the last doll's throat had been cut, perhaps?

"God Almighty," said Claire on the telephone. "There must be some mistake. There isn't a great-grandmother. My mother has been dead for years. It can't be her. I only hope it isn't someone really dangerous on the loose. I'll come over and see, just to be on the safe side. Ring the police? Yes, I think perhaps you should. But first of all make sure you've got the children well away from her."

So my dear Claire threw on a cardigan and rushed over to Linda Johnson's house with a vague irrational fear of ghosts in her mind. It couldn't possibly be her horrible tyrannical old mother returned as a *spectre* to teach little children how to chop the heads off their dolls, could it?

She went straight through Linda's kitchen with a cold feeling of dread, hardly giving herself time to exchange a greeting with her neighbour. And discovered – of course – that this supposed relative was a complete stranger and obviously suffering from senile dementia. Or something like that. The police turned up minutes after Claire, and knew immediately what it was. They had actually had a patrol car driving around for the previous two hours searching for an elderly woman with Alzheimer's who had escaped from a nearby nursing home. A car arrived in a flash, the old lady was taken away with all due care and attention, and the little children, Erin and Tom, were left in wonder at the gate watching the departure of this peculiar old great-grandmother who had come and gone again so fast in their lives.

25. Recollections from the Time of the Second Flood

IN THE MIDDLE OF April we had torrential rain again. There usually are some fairly heavy thunderstorms at this time of year, but I'd really never seen anything like this. It came cascading down, the streets were awash, lawns almost obliterated. Ancient dried-up river-channels that were no more than shallow depressions in the ground were transformed into gushing streams racing down to the lake. They're what the old Mexicans used to call *torrentes*, river-beds that only become rivers when there's a heavy downpour. They go right through whole properties, with no respect for modern changes, for houses and gardens. My neighbour who always worries so much about his lawn is rather upset, because most of his lawn soil in the front of the house has been washed into the river, which is browner and higher now than it is in the winter. And quite a lot has been deposited outside my garage like a strange sort of flood-wall so that I can't put the car away any more.

Tom!

The boy gets up and walks around at night. He's disturbed about something, and comes out of his mother's room at the end of the corridor, where he sleeps on an old folding guest-bed at the foot of hers, and wanders through the house like a little elf. Or an unquiet spirit.

I would never have discovered it if I hadn't had one of my own restless periods when I get up and walk around. Turn over a few papers in the study, say hello to the pool-cleaner (who is not quite as talkative, though, as he used to be), spend five minutes looking at some of those dreadful night-time television programmes (which frequently make me even more frightened and depressed), and attempt, with the aid of three or four sleeping tablets and a large glass of milk, to get back to sleep again.

Now, on these nocturnal perambulations, I've unexpectedly started bumping into little Tom all over the house. It quite scared me on the first occasion. He goes round with a small torch that he got from me the day we went up in the attic to seek out a toy train that was supposed to have been there at one time. He's very determined for his age, makes himself at home, does a lot of thinking, and sets out to explore this new world that he's arrived in without any active volition on his own part. I suspect that one of the things he's pondering on is his parents' divorce. But that's not a matter he'll confide to me. Otherwise we talk to each other quite a bit.

On the subject of our friends and enemies in the animal kingdom, and the death of animals: in the kitchen, since we were up and wide awake anyway (and in a morbidly humorous mood), I drew his attention to an unpleasant but interesting fact – the inordinately greater number of cockroaches there actually are in a clean and comfortable Texan house than you see during the day. They lie hidden – in cracks and crevices, in the corner behind the breadbin, under the draining board, behind the toaster. At night when they feel safe and are out hunting you can take them by surprise. You can suddenly catch one in the beam of the torch, and it will immediately stop, turn and rush off in the opposite direction. They're extremely quick insects for such a clumsy-looking body, and they're disgustingly intelligent creatures. They even have a kind of self-confidence. They seem convinced that they can escape.

I told him how I usually hunt them. I pretend to approach with the dustpan from one direction, and squash them with a fatal blow from a rolled-up newspaper from the other when they run off the wrong way. And I also showed him how they in fact guess right on more than fifty per cent of occasions. They have a kind of repulsive sensitivity for what you plan to do. If they didn't have it, of course, there would hardly be any cockroaches left in the world. I have an intense hatred of them, and pursue them to their death, which is not always easy. Sometimes you actually have to sit them out, switching off the light and pretending you've gone away.

I find it rather repugnant to pick up the corpses with my fingers, and I often use kitchen paper. It turns out to be a well-founded distaste. I read in *The New York Times* that there are thirty or so different diseases spread by cockroaches. Sometimes I throw them alive into the waste disposer, with a cruelty that I can feel surging up and emanating from me like a black cloud.

I occasionally wonder how cockroaches view me. Perhaps as a sort of horrifically cruel god who pounces on them the moment they least expect it. How do they know it's not a god they're dealing with?

In our evil designs, we always succeed. If we wish to help, we soon find that we cannot help everyone. But there is a worse stage still, when we doubt whether we can even help anyone.

Conclusions? There's a wound, a vile festering wound in the healthy, senseless surface of the world.

A person who encounters God can never be certain that it was God he encountered.

Tom seems to find that very reassuring. I don't.

Tom and I have started reading books in the evenings. The other day, when I didn't have anything else to hand, I picked up the Bible and read the story of the Tower of Babel. I was a bit worried that the little boy would find it odd – because it *is* odd. But not at all! Children love stories that give an explanation, how fish got their fins and why the monkey has a long tail. And this one explains why there are so many different countries and languages. Young Tom isn't stupid. He catches on pretty quickly, and he could see that from the very first moment in this story God appears as an enemy of humankind, an antagonist and opponent. All people speak the same language. After having been created and ejected from Eden they travel eastwards and find a valley in Shinar, where they settle. They get on well together and they build their tower. The usual old Babylonian towered city, well known to archaeologists.

Then along comes God, envious and malicious, and says: "This is just the beginning. Now nothing is impossible for them, whatever they decide to do. We [what 'we'? asks Tom, and it's really not easy to find an answer] shall go down and confound their language, so that they don't understand one another's speech."

Tom considers it a pretty mean trick, and that it can only be regarded as envy. I'd never thought about it before, but of course the little boy is quite right. This is not the way a benevolent power would talk, that's for sure. The concept is Gnostic, many centuries before Gnosticism, just like the story about the Tree of Knowledge, which is also about making human beings toe the line, mainly so that they won't start tampering with the Tree of Life. Is there an inherent Gnosticism in the oldest texts which is so obvious that nobody has really perceived it? Tom saw it straight away. Does anyone at all read these writings after Voltaire? Or do people just say they read them?

I became so interested that I looked it up in the *Encyclopaedia Judaica*. Just as I suspected. It turns out that the story of the Tower of Babel comes from the so-called J source, a different original from the main part of the text.

Is it all a joke?

Can you take seriously people who claim to know or understand these writings? Or profess to believe in them? What does it mean to believe in the story of the Tower of Babel?

Tom says he's firmly convinced that God is against us. Otherwise He would never have taken his Daddy away from him.

26. Diluvium *by Unknown Artist*

Tom and i are standing at the window watching the water rise. Claire is keeping to the kitchen because it doesn't have a window facing the river. She thinks it's frightening. There's a lot on both radio and television about the rain that's not going to stop and the huge inundations higher up the river. By Lake Travis there are apparently hundreds of people out on the promontories who have had to vacate their homes, and sailing boats have been moored to the tree-tops if their owners haven't managed to get them away by trailer. The old moorings have already been destroyed by the winter floods in any case. They say the Clubhouse is still full of mud. I find all these floods very disturbing. Are those mad fools right, perhaps, who keep on complaining about the increasing depletion of the ozone layer and climatic deterioration?

Tom, on the other hand, is enjoying it immensely. He stands at the window for hours looking at everything the river is carrying with it. We just have to make sure he doesn't go down there. And to tell the truth, even I am beginning to wonder how it's going to end, and I'm used to the worst after so many years here by the river. To start with it was mostly boats dragged loose from their moorings, but today whole trees have begun to pass by, branches, roots, the lot – and with remarkable velocity.

There's nothing left of our own jetty, except a couple of posts. And the swift brown water is forming whirlpools around them. We had hauled our boats up into the boathouse long before the rains came – after all, it's only three days to

Christmas Eve – but now it's simply a question of how long the boathouse will hold up.

Not to speak of all the jetties of various sizes that are floating past. More and more of them. You can't help wondering whether anything unusual has occurred up at Mansfield Dam. If the entire dam were to give way, which I would think totally impossible unless terrorists breached it with explosives, our house would be thirty or forty feet under within twenty minutes. That's a thought which has frankly never bothered me before. But I've actually begun to think it in the last few days.

I COULD SUDDENLY END UP THIRTY FEET UNDER WATER.

It's Saturday today; I don't need to go out before the Monday session of the Court. I hope the road will be restored by then; I've just heard from a neighbour that most of it is under water from here to the second bend.

And we could hardly get away by boat. All boat traffic is forbidden, obviously as being too perilous. They've opened six storm-gates in Mansfield Dam, according to the radio. To prevent people being drowned like rats up at Lake Travis. That's all very well, but now it's almost starting to look as if we'll be the ones to drown down here by the lower lake. And what am I doing? I'm writing. Writing something that I've been thinking about for months but haven't had enough peace and quiet to put on paper until now. It's not very easy to formulate it in words:

Anselm of Canterbury promulgated his Argument for the existence of God in 1070 in a book called *Proslogion*, and had hardly completed it before his contemporaries set about refuting it. First in the ring was the monk Gaunilo. Then they slowly followed one after the other through the centuries: Descartes, Leibnitz, Kant.

In brief, the Argument is that if God is imaginable, then God must exist. Because an existing being is better than one that doesn't exist.

That, as Kant pointed out, is utter nonsense. It's obvious that fifty dollars in my pocket are much better than fifty dollars in my imagination. But fifty dollars in my imagination don't look any different. I can even imagine them in my pocket. Existence, as we used to say in our Philosophy class in my youth, is not a property. Properties exist. Existence does not exist. I can think of plenty more good arguments against Anselm, many that I've actually never heard elsewhere. Why should it be better to exist than not to exist? It's self-evident that a virus which does not exist is better than one which exists. (What about evil people? Is an evil person who does not exist better than one who does? I have a feeling we'll soon get into a quagmire here, but no matter.) You could for example ask the question why a dog that exists should be regarded as better than one that does not exist. Or why a god who exists should be regarded as better than one who does not

I can't even see that my own existence means anything special.

A vacuum, the darkness beyond the galaxies, which Theresa's husband Anthony T. Winnicott apparently wrote about in *The Conquerors*, that fertile and scintillating vacuum must presumably be better, with all its unrealised possibilities, than this world, where everything is already realised?

The Old Man taught me and Paul and many others about this in our youth, and made a big issue of it. Something that he tried to impress upon us in particular, with a certain amount of tedious repetition, it has to be said, was that Descartes, Leibnitz and Kant were all wrong. They had only read the Argument as it was put forward in *Proslogion II*, which was not the full Argument but merely a superficial presentation. The Argument proper doesn't appear until *III* and *IV*.

God cannot do other than exist, for a god who does not exist is a self-contradictory idea. God must be a necessary idea, so to speak. God cannot exist by chance. God cannot be interchangeable with something that is exactly the same.

Cannot be something that could be copied. And cannot be something that arose by chance. Would a natural catastrophe, the origin of the Universe for instance, be able to create a god? We would not accept the chance element in such a deity. *Unfortunately*, as the Old Man used to say (and he was not very old then: it's horrible when you realise that we were listening in awe to his lectures only eleven years after he had ceased his totally different work as Nazi propagandist and writer of inflammatory anti-Semitic articles. *Only eleven years!*)

Anyone who grappled with the *proper* Argument in *Proslogion III* must sooner or later draw the right conclusion: poor old Anselm had proved the wrong God! Or, to use a more modern formulation, had proved that a biblical God could not exist, a benevolent or raging character who involved himself in the affairs of the world and who "sent a man" to the right place at the right time, could not exist. Because such a God would never meet the strict demands that Anselm makes of "a necessary being". Modern logical analysis has shown that no material object can exist of necessity. Only an abstract entity can do that.

There might perhaps be things that could not be imagined as non-existent in the world, but in that case they would be general, abstract things: forms, qualities (like extent or time) and ideas. Nothing concrete. The Greeks had in Anselm, with his abstract God, won a decisive battle, as it were, over the personal God of the Jews, but only at the price of immense dilution.

This "Being whose existence could not be imagined without its abstract concept" was not really much use. And the immanent God was from then on left to look after Himself. The question was not simply whether Anselm had gone astray in the ontological labyrinths. The question was much more painful than that: whether he hadn't in pure error gone so far as to prove that God was unimaginable.

I've thought a bit about Theresa's husband, the man who saw God, and even read a few of his books. They show talent, but don't give any real clues. What he is actually writing about throughout is what it means to be a human being, often couched in the form of ingenious stories of increasingly complex robots and other humanoids. He also writes about what it means to be a *specific individual.*

How do we know that we are? How do I know that I'm not a copy of myself? The normal problem of isolation – that's what I call it; I don't know what the philosophers call it (is what I can see the same as what you are talking about?) – is compounded enormously, it seems to me, if someone is convinced he can see God. He has to try somehow to ascertain *which* God it is that he has seen.

Theresa's husband, the madman, Mr Anthony T. Winnicott (it's odd that she's never wanted to show me a photograph of him) had undergone an experience without parallel. His reason, such as it was, had been overwhelmed by what seemed to him to be a superior, benevolent, immense intelligence. His first thought was: *Who* am I dealing with?

An indication, to my mind, that this strange man was serious.

In what was apparently his last and unfinished novel *Go Quietly! Don't Talk to the Flies!* there's a completely deranged but fine passage which goes something like this:

"The initial question to ask if one really meets what seems to be a superhuman intelligence encompassing and giving meaning to our own is of course not 'Do you exist?' or anything like that. Rather, the great burning question has to be: 'Are you the one the others meant? Or are you something completely new that no one has ever encountered before?' Angelica realised that this question could never be answered, and she resolutely rejected it."

Little Tom is jumping up and down at the window; when anything really exciting floats along he rushes over to fetch me from the dining table here where I'm sitting writing at this moment.

Do we actually need to believe all this tiresome talk about "global warming" and climatic change? Just imagine if we're really heading for a new meteorological era, with Texas having the climate of India, and a monsoon season instead of our comfortable dry winters. And cockroaches and centipedes are spreading north, I saw in the paper the other day. Large cockroaches, those little devils that I like hunting at night with Tom, are now being found in fitted carpets right up as far as Chicago. Perhaps we are moving towards a new era, where nothing balances any more. Where the big American cities will annihilate themselves and be abandoned, where altered climates will create new deserts and new agricultural areas, where none of the former rules will apply, a transition period like that between the Romans and the folk migrations? Where our rules will no longer be valid?

Oh, Theresa, how long will this river go on rising?

Why does everyone take it all so calmly? Can't they see that the world is in the process of transformation?

Tom is calling again, and this time it really was worth going to look: a complete little house – a very small one, the sort in which you keep paddles and boards, but a house nevertheless – swept past downstream at surprising speed.

"But no dead bodies yet," Tom observed, with just the slightest tinge of disappointment in his voice.

27. *Science Fiction*

I MUST SAY, IT'S starting to become unpleasant.
I suddenly feel ill at ease. Threatened on all sides. I knew that the end of April would bring a crisis. It's pressing in on me. Somebody is after me. And I know who it is.

When I returned from the courtroom, my secretary had taken no fewer than four telephone calls from a man who said he would ring again later. The message was that he *wished to sell a dog back to me.*

That afternoon with Theresa, *my one and only angel*, in her bookshop, this time after a stressful day. How small and thin she is! Such slim and supple legs! A waist that I can almost encircle with my hand!

"Have you heard any more?"

"About what?"

"About Winnicott. Your sci-fi writer."

"I haven't heard from him again. To tell the truth, it was more than three years ago when I last heard from him. I'm afraid I was telling you a little lie. I didn't want to give the impression of being too alone. He *may* be dead. But I sense that he's still alive. You probably guessed it was he who gave me this bookshop?"

"No, I hadn't realised."

"One of his books was made into a film. Suddenly he had loads of money, something that neither of us was used to."

"How did you manage before?"

(I was quite moved to feel how she almost instinctively squeezed up close to me, into my armpit, you could say, as if she were seeking protection against an evil world.)

"Badly. His books earned him practically nothing. I suspect they cheated him quite a bit. We both made silver jewellery for a while. The kind that's sold on Guadalupe Street, 'The Drag' – you know the sort of thing."

"All I know is that it's part of the drugs scene."

"You dear man, Anthony Winnicott *was* involved with drugs. He's eighteen years older than me, if he's still alive. He was part of the great ecstatic Sixties. When hallucinogens were all the rage. Not least here in Austin. Many of his friends were destroyed for life. He wasn't always easy to live with, you know. He could be incredibly paranoid sometimes. He was completely convinced that the FBI and CIA were out to get him. When one of his sci-fi colleagues was subjected to a quite reasonable tax inspection (he hadn't put in a declaration for ten years), he thought the IRS were checking up on him too. From then on he demanded payment in cash for all his books. In the end it was delivered by Federal Express, and he always hid the money here in the bookshop. 'Americans never steal books,' was what he used to say.

"No, he was unbelievably paranoid.

"I was a waitress for a while in the bar of an Italian restaurant. It was out near the airport, one those Italian pizza restaurants that have virtually nothing to do with Italy or Italians. The staff were so un-Italian that they couldn't understand what was written on their own menu. They were as Texan as their customers. But Anthony couldn't bear the idea that I worked in an Italian restaurant. He'd read about the *Banco Ambrosiano* in the newspapers, and was afraid that the Curia or the Mafia, or the Curia Mafia or whatever it is, would employ me to spy on him. He genuinely feared that the Holy Office was after him. That's probably quite an original idea, isn't it, even for a paranoid?"

"But why, for heaven's sake?"

"That was about the time he'd started conversing with God. Or at least had his feeling that there perhaps was a God – his

Gnostic God who was inimical to the God of this world – and that this God was trying to make contact with him. He became calmer later on, indeed much calmer when he received the Sign. But I had to stop working at that Italian joint, and fast. He thought it was probably in communication with Rome. And if things were as he suspected – that the official Catholic Church was presiding over a major historical falsification of what was in fact a Gnostic truth about the world – then it must be a top priority for Rome to get rid of him."

"Tell me some more about the books," I said. "*The Day the Last Human Has Died* and the others."

"Oh, there were so many," she said. "One for example was entitled *Go Quietly! Don't Talk to the Flies!* It was never published, but I've read it. It begins, I seem to recall, high up in an old tower, in a vaulted room with an ovoid ceiling. It's an ancient castle in Tuscany. It's hard to make out what the room has been used for. It might have been a torture chamber. Perhaps an alchemist's laboratory.

"Into this room come an American tourist and his wife. Her name is Angelica. She immediately says: 'But I've been in this room before.' 'Impossible,' he replies. But she insists. She has been there before. He feels frightened. They quarrel. Suddenly the wife carefully prises up a stone and takes out, as if she's always known it was there, what looks like a folded piece of paper. Her husband, afraid of God knows what, perhaps that the caretaker will come, hums and hahs and wants her to replace it. She is insistent and slowly unfolds the paper. It turns out to be so old that it's written on parchment. It contains a sequence of alchemical symbols, all the usual ones, Mars, Saturn and so forth, in a definite order and with numbers in between. Perhaps it's an astrological calculation. 'But you can't take it,' says the husband when he sees his wife about to pocket the parchment. 'Of course I can,' she responds. 'It says here that it's intended for me.' She unfolds it again. At the head of the sheet, in a fine Italian hand, are the words: '*Angelica B. Smith, on her arrival at Castello.*'

"What ideas! And it continues in roughly the same style. He had masses. *Don't Talk to the Flies* is just a fragment – it's not easy to see what direction he was going in. But he always had that originality about him. There is for instance an uncompleted story called *The Conquerors* that takes place somewhere out in deepest space and is totally polytheistic. The world is created not by one but by many gods, who are all at war with one another. The great natural forces are utterly impossible to unite in one single formula – as Einstein wanted – simply because they have absolutely nothing to do with one another. A primordial and long-vanquished god created gravity and thus laid the basis for younger usurpers to introduce electromagnetic energy. From a world composed only of plasma a third group of gods created solid states by introducing the strong and weak interaction that made atomic particles possible. Now a new god is in the process of forming himself out there in the vacuum, that luminous and fertile vacuum far beyond the galaxies; he is preparing himself to be the next conqueror and will probably bring in entirely new natural laws with entirely new and incomprehensible states and developments.

"The Universe consists of the archaeological relics of the gods, and every new conqueror has to be content with building on the old. And the old powers do all they can to hinder the new one who is trying to force his way in from the outer reaches of the vacuum.

"Yes, that was an idea that could have made an interesting book. After he started earning a little money from his novels and didn't necessarily have to produce one a month, he had a tendency to begin with very good ideas but never finish them. I don't really know why that was. He was tremendously restless. *The Conquerors* was the last one he was working on before he received the Sign and disappeared. After he'd had the Sign he was perceptibly calmer, almost happy. Like a different man, you could say. The paranoia vanished altogether. As if he no longer had that peculiar need to convince himself that he was being watched. If you read his books, you can see that this belief in being watched is there as a theme too. All the time."

"Where did he go?"

She cuddled up even closer to me on the narrow, threadbare sofa. Outside there was an unusually clear and distinct song thrush in the tree, but it was almost drowned out by a police siren that must have been approaching along Thirty-Fifth Street. It's never really quiet in this city, I thought. Where do you have to go to find total silence?

"*He wanted to go somewhere where he could find total silence*, he always said. I don't know whether that meant death or a remoter part of Arizona or Washington State. Quite honestly I'm not sure that I'm particularly worried any longer. I've had about all I can take of Anthony T. Winnicott. You're not as crazy, are you? You're a completely normal man, aren't you?"

She stroked my cheek cautiously.

"What actually was that *Sign*?"

"I don't know. He never managed to describe it in an intelligible way. Or rather, he described it in a different way every time. Sometimes it sounded as if he was talking about an epileptic fit, and on other occasions it was more as if he had hit upon a kind of principle. A principle that wasn't easy to explain but that obviously made the world meaningful for him. He felt the way a passage of text in a book might feel if it discovered that it was in a book. Do you understand what I mean?"

"No. I can't say I do. But never in my whole life have I wished so fervently to understand anything as I do this."

28. The Evil Magician

LITTLE TOM HAS GOT several young friends in the neigh-
bourhood now; with due permission, he has been playing basketball at the Johnsons' house at the upper end of the
street, a nice family who seem to attract children from all
around. Perhaps because the adults in the family are friendly
and always willing to join in and play. And they've got a
special low basket for children, so that everyone has a fair
chance of netting the ball. The Johnsons' own children, three
little girls, are Erin, Vicky and Elsie. Elsie, the smallest, has
just had her third birthday and was allowed to invite all her
friends. Including Tom.

Right up to the last minute I was afraid that Tom's mother
would find some radical or poststructuralist or feminist argument against birthdays, I mean with cakes and ice creams
and *piñata* (those little paper men you hang on trees and that
children hit with a stick till sweets pour out of their violently
ruptured bodies). But it transpired that children's parties
actually had her ideological approval.

She had nothing against it, provided that I went with him.
She herself had found some kind of women's circle that meets
on Sunday afternoons on the campus. So I went. There are
always a few adults to talk to at a children's party after all, if
you can get a word in between all the admonitions and nose-
wiping and peace negotiations that have to go on. And these
were my neighbours, even if my generation, the grandfathers'
generation, was not as well represented as those of the
children and grandchildren. Good Lord, I thought as I saw

some of the tall, slender, stylish and fit upper-class women tending their little darlings, Good Lord, it isn't long since I saw those very mothers going down the street on their tricycles. I probably even saved one or two of them from losing their lives under an approaching dustcart.

Twenty to twenty-five years ago.

Tom was very enthusiastic about the whole thing from the outset; he held my hand in his own always rather excited hand the entire way. Because he'd heard there would be a magician. Around here there has to be either a pony or a magician at children's birthday parties. The pony is the same one nearly every time, carefully – no, lethargically – led round the lawn by a very reliable man called Jimmy, or some name like that. I think we had him occasionally when Tom's mother was young. Both the pony and Jim seemed indestructible.

Magicians are a more unreliable species. When my children were small there was at least one who used to fortify himself from a hip-flask in the wings between performances. Another I remember would smell so strongly of cigarette smoke that you had to recoil when you came to pay him his twenty dollars or whatever it cost in those days. He was one of the most skilful magicians. He used to phone a few days in advance and ask whether the family happened to keep rabbits. If they did, a string of rabbits would pop out of his hat, rabbits that looked so ordinary and familiar until this artful and oddly nervous chain-smoker started transforming them into doves, large blue doves that to the children's delight would flutter right out into the room. (And leave a good few traces on the carpet.)

I can't say that I go to children's parties all that often nowadays. The one with Tom must have been the first for a great many years.

In fact, this event took quite a strange turn. The magician, somewhat pallid and hollow-cheeked, with spectacles and a rather obstinate pointed beard, seemed a bit peculiar. His equipment appeared to be endless, and before he'd finished bringing in his cases and setting up his dark-blue backcloth in the Johnsons' living room, the children were getting terribly restive as they sat in an expectant group on the carpet. Tom was sitting right in the front with an unusually frail little boy, who may have had a minor handicap that I couldn't see properly from behind, where I was sitting – asthma perhaps, or slight brain-damage – anyway, Tom sat holding the other child by the hand the whole time. As if he needed to be protected in some way. He was making tiny agitated movements, jerking his head from side to side at irregular intervals, almost as if he were trying to shake off something that was annoying him.

The magician went through his routine: all the old familiar tricks, cards that changed colour, rabbits that turned into doves and doves that became rabbits again, and scarves that turned up as a long string of American flags. He did it all with a rather preoccupied, faintly aggressive energy which evidently irritated the adults a bit as they sat in the background endeavouring to summon up a show of indulgent interest. The children were also affected: they were noticeably exhilarated, rather too much so. And they giggled in the pauses, when there actually wasn't much to giggle at.

Something was slightly wrong, but it wasn't easy to say exactly what. It was in the air.

The climax of these performances at children's birthday parties tends to consist of the magician inflating and twisting together superb figures of multi-coloured balloons, animals, swords, funny-shaped hats. So now all the children stood in a queue, stamping in their eagerness to get at the balloons he was blowing up and twisting and knotting for them, one after another. You couldn't deny that he made them in a highly ingenious way, and they poured out into the room with a kind of dreary precision. The children danced around with them gleefully.

Eventually it was the turn of Tom and his new friend, the frail little boy whose hand he was still clasping.

I couldn't believe my eyes when the magician, unexpectedly,

but very firmly and as if it were a matter of course, waved them back to the end of the queue. What was going on? Had the boys pushed themselves forward in some way? Was that the reason, and now they had to be punished?

They waited patiently in the queue once more, and all the children received balloons, some even a second. But as soon as my little friends reached the front again, the magician waved them away: no balloons left.

He couldn't do anything about it. Gone! When they're gone, they're gone! He wiped his empty hands together demonstratively. The frail boy burst into inconsolable tears. Tom, who can really be a fine little fellow, put both his arms round him as if to protect him.

I couldn't see that it was anything but a totally *heinous* act of bullying, of meaningless brutality, of thorough evil to which I had been a silent witness. But none of the other adults seemed to have noticed it; on the contrary, they were talking appreciatively to the evil magician after his satanic performance. And the frail little boy was still sobbing uncontrollably. When his mother, one of the fit and slender young tennis-players who inhabit the area, arrived later to fetch her son, she couldn't understand what had happened. And she wouldn't listen to my polite attempts to explain; she was one of those modern people brought up with the TV thundering out in the living room day and night who have quite lost the ability to hear what other people are saying.

I offered to take both boys to a good toyshop on Exposition Boulevard on the other side of the river, Ultimate Toys, to fix them up with a few balloons. The mother rejected the suggestion without making any attempt at politeness herself. All she wanted was to take her troublesome, disconsolate child away.

What should be done about the evil magician? I'd actually considered telling him a few home truths, at the risk of appearing to lose my temper or even of being eccentric, but by the time I'd come to the end of my fruitless efforts to make myself understood by the boy's mother, the devil had already packed up and disappeared.

The awful thing was that I had such a distinct, spine-chilling sensation of a really evil person. Another time he'll murder a child. I know it.

What was it about him that reminded me of The Most Intelligent Man? There wasn't the slightest physical resemblance: any similarity was more in my reactions. There are people who arouse in me an almost insane rage; not the fraudsters, swindlers, thieving bank-directors or disloyal colleagues on the bench – no, not them! That's more human nature. It's the blinkered, cold people who go straight through the world as if it weren't there and trample over everything in their path, simply because they don't see it. No. That's not right either – it's hard to explain this, even to myself. Their greatest crime is that they don't see me. But that sounds crazy! Am I really so self-centred? That's wrong too. That's not what I have to reproach them with. They project the same cold indifference towards everybody. But I happen to be the one who can perceive it.

(A bizarre thought that may indicate that I am going mad: what if this is *some kind of new species*, that's in the process of silently invading us? *Bodysnatchers* – as they were called in that old science-fiction film. *The Most Intelligent Man* and *The Evil Magician* have something in common, but I can't for the life of me work out what it is. If I come across another example, I'll start to believe in the idea! This is exactly the kind of theory, moreover, that would definitely have interested Theresa's poor husband. I mean, for the type of science fiction, metaphysical and unique, that he wrote. I wonder whether he's still alive?)

On the way home with Tom, still puzzled and asking why, out of all the children, the magician wouldn't give a balloon to him and Willie, it occurred to me that I could easily have obtained from my hosts the evil man's visiting card with his name and address. You never know what might happen.

Thank God I'm not District Attorney – I think I would prosecute people just according to my intuition.

"That," I said to Tom, "that was a really evil person. They're actually quite rare. There are slightly wicked people everywhere. But the thoroughly evil ones are so few and far between that not everybody has the misfortune to meet one in a lifetime."

"Like rattlesnakes?"

"Even rarer," I replied. "Considerably rarer. But just as real."

29. *A Card Laid Is a Card Played*

A T THE BEGINNING I had no idea he hated me so much. I mean of course my real enemy, Mr Douglas Melvin Smith, at this point in time the most intelligent man in the USA.

They came somewhat irregularly at first, and then at exactly weekly intervals. I'm talking – as everyone will obviously understand – about the postcards from The Most Intelligent Man.

Sometimes they came to the house, and sometimes to the Court office, and I didn't think much about them when they started. A few of them were entirely inoffensive, one post-marked in San Antonio and another in Cincinnati. (He appeared to travel from place to place with astonishing speed. Occasionally he seemed to move between locations as far apart as Anchorage, Alaska, Taos in New Mexico and the Cayman Islands in the Caribbean all on the same day. As if he had a private jet at his disposal. Or as if he had associates he could ask to post the cards.) The greetings were extremely trivial and the views didn't match the place of origin. The one from Cincinnati was clearly a reprint of a Berlin street scene of the early Thirties. There was a gleaming silver cigar floating above the canal: an airship.

But the most frequent were the cards from Galveston. A rhythm gradually established itself (I have a note of it, since everything that comes by post to the Court is precisely recorded): a card every third week. Was it the earliest cards that were aggressive? I think so. It rather depends on what we mean by "aggressive". What counts as aggressive is a cultural phenomenon, says one of my assistants, an intelligent but unfortunately temporary colleague in whom I've confided. (Not entirely, but to some extent.)

A *bull*, the sort of picture postcard that is to be found in every stationer's and grocer's in West Texas, the longhorn steer. They have this strange cult of the bull. You might think they were original early Jews: they too had an allusion to the bull, that golden calf they raised on a pole to celebrate the return of Moses (with horns on his head) from the Mountain with the Tablets of the Law. I saw it all as a boy in Doré's illustrations and didn't understand a thing. But we all know Bevo, the bull-calf, here in Austin, the mascot of the University football team, a fine and very masculine little animal who is led round the field in almost ritual fashion before every match of the season. Oh yes! Our friends the animals are all around us! If you think about it carefully enough, they seem to be almost standing in a circle staring at us.

This bull didn't speak. He arrived with absolute regularity every week. There was nothing whatsoever on the reverse. Apart from my address. Always that of the Court. This bull stood completely still, and yet it almost appeared as if on each occasion he had taken another step towards me. The others didn't see it, but I did. (And on a less visible plane, took certain steps of my own.) So many of them have come now that my secretary has begun to wonder where to put them.

I suggested creating a special file, marked MIM – for the time being. You never know what might turn up. It's patently obvious that I must have offended the man deeply and that he has placed things on a war footing.

"You never know," I said.

"No," said my secretary. "You never know. Strange things do happen. All the time, in fact."

Then the rhythm was abruptly broken. A total surprise, just as I'd got used to this unusual attention. Suddenly, there was a card of the Tower of London. Presumably found in a second-hand bookshop, because the card made no secret of the fact that it was printed in 1951. It was sepia-toned and I would guess that tourists bought it then, in 1951, with a mixture of pleasure and horror. There was a realism about that card in 1951, so soon after the Second World War and all its gruesome events.

The card depicted the block at the Tower. Yes, the real old executioner's block with the mighty half-moon-shaped axe firmly embedded in the wood of the block.

But now the final straw.

Yesterday.

At 8.30 in the morning, just as the Court Usher was about to strike the hammer on the bench and the two parties were rising for my entrance, I saw an unfranked envelope addressed to *US Bankruptcy Judge Erwin Caldwell* lying on the bench in front of me. Since it's difficult to put things in your pocket when wearing the black gown, I left it where it was.

I don't need to open any more.

It's disconcerting enough anyway.

For I know now where I've seen these postcards before. Both the airship over Berlin and the grim executioner's axe are hanging right in front of your eyes as you enter Theresa's bookshop. Mr Douglas Melvin Smith has evidently been there in the last few days and stocked up on them.

How much does he actually know about me? How far is he willing to go to injure me? I can imagine myself beginning to feel a slight panic coming on. And in the wake of that panic, something that might be the germ of an action.

30. *The End of the Argument*

I'D KNOWN FOR A few hours that the solution would come the next day. That it would come soon, and that it would not surprise me unduly. What happened was that I received, totally unexpectedly and without any effort on my own part, some information from the inside, "insider information" as it's called nowadays.

I was somewhat taken aback to see the District Attorney in such a quiet place as the Café Mozart. He and his advisers took up an entire table, which for such a cramped room is saying quite a lot. The usual customers were blue-rinsed ladies from Tarrytown who spent whole mornings playing tennis in expensive brands of tennis skirts, or gossiping with one another in cafés. They're all the same little blonde girls who made a hit at school dances in our youth. And now they're in their forties they look confusingly alike in their artificial girlishness, their slightly alcoholic red cheeks, their eye-shadow, and the hard tight lines around their mouths that bear witness to their erotic disappointments.

Otherwise not a soul, and particularly nobody from Downtown. That was why I'd arranged to meet Theresa here. She didn't turn up, and I still don't know why. She's not answering the telephone. Nor are any of her student staff. I haven't had time to drive by and see whether the shop is open or closed. But something is odd. In fact, when I think about it, I haven't seen her for ten whole days. When I sat down, I found I'd got the table next to the District Attorney, a tall, slim, gentle, priest-like man whom I'd known since he was a young Democratic member of our House of Representatives. Very much against the Vietnam War at the time and very radical. He has retained the priestly nature. Perhaps the radical too.

His colleagues came sauntering in, one after the other: the Deputy Chief of Police and the Sheriff and the Detective Superintendent. I suspect they weren't exactly overjoyed to see me there. It was obvious that if they'd made the effort to come all the way up from the police station to this remote ladies' café, it was hardly because they were looking forward to having a judge, even if only a bankruptcy judge, as an interested audience at the adjacent table.

They seemed, however, to be completely preoccupied with their own problems, which they began discussing in animated but subdued tones. Internal intrigues, I would have said. It reeked of internal plots even at a distance: someone was going to get the sack. The Chief of Police at a guess. They don't last long nowadays. Which is fine, because they have an uncomfortable tendency to pick up far too many secrets about what's going on in town. And not just the secrets of criminals. Even the secrets of the great and the good.

No one could have been less inquisitive than I was. But I nevertheless had time for a not entirely uninteresting conversation with Tony, as he's called, our excellent, effective and also very human District Attorney. From that, and from what I heard on the news later – the D.A. naturally had plenty of gruesome details that didn't appear on television or in the papers – but anyway, as I understood it, they'd found him on a hillside in the woods on this side of the lake, but much higher up than where we live. It must have been eight or nine hundred feet higher, by one of the tracks. A north-facing slope descending into the gorge of a stream. I know it very well; there used to be chanterelle mushrooms growing there at least ten years ago.

Anyone who wasn't familiar with the area wouldn't believe it, but there are actually quite a few places here in the Hill

Country where lots of chanterelles grow. They never get as big as up in Washington State (where people are also much more aware of them, and they're picked and sold and nobody believes they cause hallucinations). They come just in the first few days of June or at the end of May, so you have to watch out for them. They grow on exactly that kind of northern slope where the early mists lie a little longer on sunny spring mornings.

Well, they obviously don't know who he was, or possibly they have no wish to say anything to the general public at this stage of the investigation. That's understandable.

But I know.

He was sitting on a wooden chair, to the seat and back of which someone had bound him with strong rope of the type you get on sailing boats, or on boats in general. A gag had been stuffed in his mouth and was soaked in some substance, probably chloroform, which had killed him. Whether this gag had been intended to kill him or whether his death was inadvertent was not easy to say. He had apparently been hurled down the hill sitting on the chair. Yet another of these ghastly, brutal crimes that have upset everyone so much over the last six months. After the murder of the three girls in the yoghurt shop, and the poor girl who was snatched from the car-wash, she too almost certainly murdered, people had thought things would calm down for a while.

Ten years ago this was a quiet and tranquil area. Of course there were crimes, but hardly on that scale, nor so close together. Yes indeed, cruelty has great reserves. It's as if it drew secret strength from a cruel god.

How do I know that it was The Most Intelligent Man, Mr Douglas Melvin Smith? Elementary, my dear Watson; elementary, my dear District Attorney. Elementary, because his great piles of papers were scattered all around him, the sheets of Lullean diagrams. All those remarkable circles, rotating around each other. How do I know that? The D.A. told me in the Café Mozart. And then there was something else too . . . something I should have said but which I keep forgetting. Yes, of course: I think I've *finally* made sense of the *Argument*! This is what has occurred to me:

The Most Intelligent Man in the United States must exist. For the existence of the most intelligent presupposes that no one more intelligent exists. If therefore he does not exist, he cannot be the most intelligent. And if he is the most intelligent, he is so if, and only if, he exists. A most intelligent man who does not exist is just not conceivable. The most intelligent man in the United States is an imaginable concept. Therefore The Most Intelligent Man exists.

I think that this, as things now stand, is a *joke in appallingly bad taste*. Nevertheless in some peculiar way it cheers me up. I think I'll phone Theresa and tell her as soon as she's back home again. From her journey.

He was called Mr Douglas Melvin Smith. Nothing else.

31. The Tortoise Always Arrives
Before Achilles

I DROVE NANCY AND Tom to the airport a week ago this
morning. Nothing has been quite the same since. It's
lonely and boring here and I have the feeling that all the people
who interested me have suddenly gone away. And I'm somehow absent from myself. I'm dry and empty and the secret fire
is no longer raging within me. (Is it true then that demons can
come just to visit you and then depart?)

I find myself displaying quiet idiocies of a totally new kind.
Invite a habit in, and it will soon settle down and make itself
at home.

I've started tidying the magazines on the table in front of
the living-room sofa, something I've never ever bothered about
before. *The New Yorker* on its own with its crazy cheerful
covers, *The American Bar Journal* between *Texas Monthly* and
The New York Review of Books. It looks a lot neater already,
almost like a library. Perhaps this way I'll find more time to
read them too?

I miss Tom. I really do. I fought to the end to have little
Tom stay on here for the time being. That is, until she'd sorted
out her situation, one way or another. I'd even phoned the
Montessori School in Alpine Road, where I have an old
contact, to see if I could find a place. They had one. It was
all arranged. He could have had a lift every day with a woman
in the next block who has children at the same school. He
could have slept in the room between Claire's and mine,
and could have come running in to one or the other of us at
night when he had disturbing dreams, as he has been doing

over these last few summer weeks. I thought I had surmised correctly that this was what Tom wanted. It was very hard having to part with him. As a leaving present he gave me a little magpie feather that he'd found in the garden. I saw his small pale face looking back at us, before he disappeared down the passageway to the Boston plane. His mother was pulling him along as if she was much more certain to know what he needed and what was awaiting him than anybody else.

This sudden desire for order won't leave me in peace. I've been down in the cellar rearranging all my fishing tackle. Hung fly-rods on one set of hooks and spinning-rods on another, put wobblers and spoon-bait and flies in different plastic drawers, untangled the old tapered fishing lines, and even suspended the canoe on two ropes from the roof. Canoes ought to hang, not stand on bits of timber in the middle of the cellar. My father taught me that. It's such a brief period of the year that you can use canoes on the river nowadays. It's really only a few days around Christmas and New Year when the motorboat traffic ceases. I tidy obsessively, and yet I'm still constantly finding new things in my cellar to sort out.

Now, a week after Nancy and Tom had left, I found the tortoise in her box. Dead as a doornail and covered in ants that had already eaten her to the bone. In fact it was only the shell and a small rattling pile of bones that remained.

I think she had been trying right to the very end to climb out, but couldn't manage the steep sides. We had put her there after breakfast on the last day, Tom and I, so that she wouldn't crawl off under the fence while I was driving him and his mother to the airport. The intention of course was that I should let her out as soon as I got back, so that she would be able to carry on her normal little garden life. But since Tom wasn't there any more, the tortoise probably no longer had so much reality for me.

At first I hadn't realised that it was our tortoise. That's how dried up it was. The shell dead and lacklustre, its tiny extremities transformed into skeletal remains by thousands of savage ants, its eyes nothing but empty sockets. With flies still crawling everywhere. In all its smallness, in its cardboard-like, dried-up insignificance, it was a significant reminder of the void of death, of *the enormous insult* it implies: that we can turn into nothing. And just because someone has stopped loving us.

How could I forget it so completely! I must have somehow imagined that the poor innocent creature had ceased to exist just because Tom went away. If I ever write to him I'll have to lie, make up adventures for a poor ant-eaten, wretched tortoise whose final hours in a box must have been an inferno. How much unnecessary suffering can this world hold before it's satisfied? Perhaps it's like that peculiar book title that Theresa's husband, the forgotten science-fiction author, wrote: "The Day the Last Human Being Has Died, the Whole Solar System Will Feel So Much Freer and Happier"?

Evening news. Autumn darkness. Grey herons sitting motionless for ages in the trees by the river. Far too many grey herons. They're starting to be pests. Nothing pleasant at all. But at last a breakthrough in these murders that have really disturbed us all so much throughout the autumn. I felt a deep sense of moral satisfaction when I heard it on the news: they've caught the man now. A sex maniac who had been sentenced to life imprisonment but was freed experimentally in the Seventies. They found him in Oregon in one of those parks for mobile homes where he'd apparently been living for the last six months. He'd been supporting himself from refuse disposal and it was obviously pure chance that they stopped him and found he didn't have a valid driving licence. It appeared that he'd already been connected with a series of unusual murders in Travis County. Though I wasn't in the habit of phoning him, I rang up my old friend Tony, the D.A., and he said that there was no end to all the things the man had been confessing to. A young woman, disappeared without trace from a car-wash, three girls shot just before closing time in a yoghurt shop. Most of the instances, particularly in some of the details of his methods, Tony and I agreed, point to his also being the perpetrator of the meaningless and horrific murder of the inoffensive person who called himself The Most Intelligent Man. Who else would have wished him ill?

The awful thing is that this murderer they've now found was jailed in the Sixties for several similar crimes of insanity, but was set free after only seven years by some insane parole board. Ah well. Politics have changed since then. This time he's not likely to get out so easily.

I feel a great moral satisfaction myself, a sense of relief that the murderer of The Most Intelligent Man will be brought to justice and tried. Strange as it may sound, I had a very bad conscience as far as he was concerned. He hated me and was persecuting me with his stupid threats about the dog. How he could have known anything about the affair of the dog was and will remain a mystery. I sometimes toy with the thought that I was actually the one who told him, that summer afternoon when we met. But it would have been so bizarre that I have to discount the notion. Perhaps there was however a tiny, tiny element of truth in his belief that I had ruined his life.

It wasn't entirely necessary to warn those female students about him. On the other hand, they could have been in danger. It was just that it was so utterly impossible to take him seriously. To have had him as a friend must have been even worse than having him as an enemy.

(I really didn't grieve for that repulsive dog. I do grieve for this little animal. Yes, for the first time in this story I feel something that has a remote affinity to a guilty conscience. But it doesn't help you, you poor tortoise, of all forsaken creatures!

How frighteningly high the walls of the box must have towered above you as the days went by and your thirst grew to be a searing fire in your desiccated little body. Taller and taller the sides must have seemed against an empty and impregnable blue sky, and a thirst that nothing more could quench.)